The Rescued Puppy

and other tales

The Rescued Puppy

and other tales

by Holly Webb

Illustrated by Sophy Williams

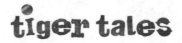

tiger tales

5 River Road, Suite 128, Wilton, CT 06897
Published in the United States 2020
Text copyright © Holly Webb
The Rescued Puppy 2011
The Tiniest Puppy originally published as
Lucy the Poorly Puppy 2011
The Abandoned Puppy 2013
Illustrations copyright © Sophy Williams
The Rescued Puppy 2011
The Tiniest Puppy 2011
The Abandoned Puppy 2013
ISBN-13: 978-1-68010-478-3
ISBN-10: 1-68010-478-0
Printed in the USA
STP/4800/0383/0920
10 9 8 7 6 5 4 3 2

For more insight and activities, visit us at www.tigertalesbooks.com

Contents

The Rescued Puppy

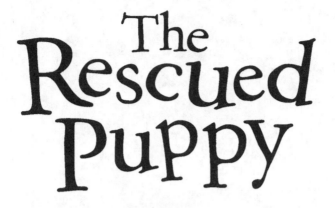

Contents

For Ethan and Harry

Chapter One
Cooper's First Walk

"I still think the blue leash was better," Alex said, staring down at Cooper's new leash with his arms folded and a sulky expression on his face.

"No, red looks great with his fur. If you hadn't spent all your money on candy, you could have bought the new leash!" Becky pointed out. "This is Cooper's first walk. Do you want Mom to say we can't go because we're fighting? She will, you know!"

"Oh, all right…," Alex muttered. Then he grinned at his twin sister. "I don't think you're going to be able to get the leash on him, anyway!"

Cooper, Becky and Alex's cocker spaniel puppy, was dancing around Becky's feet, squeaking and yipping with excitement.

"Cooper, hold still!" Becky giggled, trying to hook the leash onto his collar. "Look, we won't ever get to take a walk if you won't let me clip this on!"

"Are you two ready yet?" Mom came into the hallway. "Where are we going for this special walk?"

"The park!"

"The woods!"

Becky and Alex spoke at the same time, and Mom sighed. "I think Alex's probably got the better idea this time, Becks. The woods might be too tiring for Cooper on his first big walk. The paths are so narrow, and Cooper would be scrambling over fallen trees and things. Let's get him used to something easier first."

Becky sighed. "I guess. I bet he'll love the woods when he's bigger, though. Oooh!" Quickly she clipped the leash onto Cooper's collar, while the puppy was distracted, looking at Mom. "There! Now we're ready!"

Cooper pulled excitedly at the new leash, twirling himself around Becky's ankles. He had been on a leash before, for his trips to the vet and the puppy parties he'd been to in order to get used to other dogs, but it was still very exciting. He could feel that Becky and Alex were excited about something, too, and he couldn't stop jumping up and down.

Alex and Becky had gotten Cooper two months before, as a joint ninth birthday present. They had been trying for a while to persuade their parents to get a dog, but Mom and Dad had only just decided that they were old enough. Luckily, Becky and Alex had agreed that they would really love a spaniel— one of their friends at school, Max, had a beautiful black cocker spaniel named Jet, and they both loved to play with him when Max's mom brought him to pick up Max after school.

Becky and Alex's mom had asked where Jet had come from, and Max's mom had given her the name of the rescue center. She told them the puppies were all very well taken care of and used to children. But when Becky and Alex's mom called, there was only one 10-week-old puppy left. Alex and Becky had their hearts set on a spaniel, so the whole family had driven over to see him right away.

At first, all they could see was the puppy's mom, lying on a fluffy blanket. She was the most beautiful golden and white spaniel, with the longest, silkiest ears they'd ever seen.

"Oh, wow...," Becky breathed. "Can we pet her?"

Laura, one of the rescue workers, nodded. "Just gently, though. You have to be careful with mother dogs when they have their puppies with them."

Alex frowned. "But she doesn't— I can't see a puppy!"

Becky grabbed his hand. "Look!" she said in an excited whisper. "I just saw him—he's fast asleep, snuggled up right next to her. He's beautiful!"

Alex leaned over. "I thought that

was his mom's tail," he admitted. "He's really cute. And tiny!"

Laura laughed. "You should have seen him when he first came to us right after he was born. He isn't really that small; to be honest, I think his mom is sitting on him."

Becky knelt down to get a closer look. "Yes, she is. Doesn't he mind?"

"No, he's all warm and cozy. He likes being the only puppy left—it means he gets all the attention, from his mom and us. He's going to want a lot of cuddles if you take him home."

Alex and Becky exchanged grins. That sounded perfect.

Just then, the little dog sighed, yawned, and opened his eyes. He looked at his mother and wriggled his bottom indignantly to tell her to get off of him. Then he heaved himself up and looked around, his tail wagging shyly. Who were all these people staring at him?

"Oh, he's so beautiful…," Becky whispered, then turned to her mom and dad. "Look at him! Isn't he perfect?"

He really was like a perfect mini

version of his mom, curly ears and all. He was golden and white, with white patches on his back and a scatter of sweet brownish-gold spots around his shiny black nose. His eyes were almost black, too, and very bright and curious-looking, topped off with long whiskery eyebrows that made him look like a little old man.

Everyone had agreed that he was the perfect puppy, and Laura had said that they could come back and take him home the very next day. It was a few weeks before Becky and Alex's birthday, but they didn't mind having their present early. As Becky pointed out the next day, as they carefully carried the puppy out of the rescue to put him into the new pet carrier in the back of the car, they were lucky to have him at all. If they had waited any longer, there might not have been any puppies left.

"And he's lucky to have us, too," Alex said. "I bet he wouldn't have liked anybody else as much. Oof!" He laughed and wiped off a smear of dog drool as the puppy gave him a wet kiss across his chin.

Soon Alex and Becky couldn't imagine not having Cooper. He was very friendly, and played endless games of chase and fetch with them in the yard. He loved running so much that he'd bound up and down, and then just suddenly flop down on the grass and fall asleep, absolutely worn out. Becky called it his "off button"; it made her burst out laughing every time.

But although Cooper loved running around in the yard, Alex and Becky had learned that cocker spaniels shouldn't really go for walks until they are about four or five months old. Alex had read it in the book they'd bought, and on a special cocker spaniel website. Becky hadn't believed him at first.

"Why not?" she'd demanded.

Alex had shrugged. "It says they love long walks when they're older—a lot of long walks—but you shouldn't wear them out too much when they're little. Just exercise in the yard."

Now that they had Cooper, Becky could understand why both the website and the book had suggested it. Cooper was still quite a small dog, but he was getting heavy. If they'd gone on a long walk and he'd switched off like he did when they were playing, he'd be a real armful to carry all the way home. But now that he was almost five months old, he wasn't getting quite as tired, and Mom and Dad agreed that he was ready for a real walk, just as long as they were careful not to go too far.

Luckily, the park was close enough

that they'd be able to carry the puppy home if he did get really worn out.

Alex opened the front door, and Cooper sniffed the air outside. The front yard smelled different than the back— more cars, and there was definitely a cat hanging around somewhere. He looked up at Becky hopefully. Were they going out?

She laughed at his eager little face. "Come on!"

Alex ran down the path to open the gate, and Cooper gave an excited squeak.

"Try and remember not to let him pull!" Mom called as she locked the front door and hurried after them. Becky and Alex had started bringing Cooper to puppy obedience classes soon after they brought him home. They'd spent a lot of time working on walking to heel, but Cooper was so excited at going somewhere new that there wasn't much chance of him doing that now.

"Oh, yes." Becky quickly grabbed a dog treat out of her pocket and held it in front of Cooper's nose, moving it back so that he was standing by the side of her leg, just as she'd practiced in the puppy obedience classes. Then she walked on down the path, and gave Cooper the treat as he trotted nicely alongside her.

"We can run with him in the park, though, can't we?" Alex asked Mom. "I don't mean we'll let him off the leash; I know he's not old enough for that. But can we run fast with him?"

"Of course you can!" Mom smiled. "It's just best to try and keep him calm on the way there. We can't expect Cooper to be perfect, though; it's all so different from our yard at home."

But Cooper had stopped wanting to dance around, anyway. He was much too busy for that. When he'd gone out for rides in the car before, to puppy training and visits to see friends, he'd always been carried. There was so much more to see down at nose level now! To see and thoroughly sniff.

Becky giggled as they stopped at the seventh lamppost—still on their road. "You know, if we want to be back by dinnertime, I'm not sure we're going to make it to the park!"

Chapter Two
A Day at the Park

They only made it just inside the park gates on that first walk before Cooper started to drag on his leash and look up hopefully to be carried. Becky and Alex took turns carrying the weary puppy home.

But over the next few weeks, a short walk every day soon stretched into two short walks, and then a quick run around the houses before breakfast and a longer walk after school, in the park or the woods. By the time Becky and Alex left school for summer vacation, walks were Cooper's absolute favorite thing.

They celebrated the beginning of vacation by taking a picnic lunch with them to the woods. It was a beautiful, hot day, perfect for a long expedition. Mom took a lawn chair so she could sit down with a book while Becky, Alex, and Cooper raced around the woods, shouting and calling and playing hide-and-seek among the tree roots.

Cooper adored the woods. They were full of amazing smells, good places to dig, and sticks that Becky and Alex could throw for him to chase. He had an extending leash now, as no one was sure about letting him run free just yet. But the absolute best thing about the woods was that they were full of squirrels. Cooper adored squirrels. They were fast, and they smelled interesting, and they bounced up and down when they scampered along. He was desperate to catch one. He'd never gotten anywhere near, but he wasn't giving up hope. And there was a squirrel now….

Alex raced behind Cooper, laughing as the puppy pulled the leash out to its full length and galloped down the path, ears flapping as if he were about to take off. The squirrel was a plump, bushy-tailed one, and it wasn't scared. It seemed to keep looking back to see how close the puppy was getting.

"Alex!" Becky yelled worriedly. "Don't

let him catch it! He'll hurt it! Or it might scratch him!"

But Alex was too far away to hear—or he just wasn't listening, Becky thought angrily as she dashed after them. She really didn't want Cooper to hurt the squirrel.

But when she caught up with Alex and Cooper, she saw that she had worried for nothing. Alex was leaning against a tree, panting, and Cooper was jumping up and down and scratching at the trunk, whimpering.

The squirrel was sitting on a branch halfway up, squeaking and chittering as though it were scolding Cooper.

"Didn't you hear me yelling?" Becky demanded. "What do you think he'd do if he caught it?"

Alex shook his head and shrugged. "No idea! I don't think he knows, either. Calm down, Becky! He's never going to get one."

Cooper ignored them, staring hopefully up at the squirrel as it danced up and down on its branch. Unfortunately, it didn't look as though it were going to fall off.

By the time they trailed back to the clearing where Mom was sitting, they were all really hungry. They had brought Cooper's dog biscuits with them, and a bottle of water and his bowl so he could have a picnic, too. He wolfed down the biscuits in about two seconds, and then stood staring at Alex's tuna sandwiches as if he were starving.

Becky giggled. "You should learn to like egg salad, Alex. He never wants my sandwiches."

Alex shuddered. "Yuck."

Mom slipped her cardigan off her shoulders, enjoying the sun. "Just think, this time next week we'll be on vacation in Seaside, California!"

Becky opened her chips and sneakily fed a very small one to Cooper. He wasn't really supposed to have them, but she couldn't resist those big, hopeful dark eyes.

"We've never been on vacation with a dog before," Alex said happily, stretching himself out on the blanket.

"It's right by the ocean, isn't it?" Becky asked again. She already knew it was—she'd seen the photos in the vacation cottage brochure—but she liked to hear her mom say it.

Mom smiled at her. "Right next to it, Becks. A little cottage just at the top of a cliff."

"And we'll be allowed to take Cooper for walks, all by ourselves?" Alex pushed himself up on his elbows.

"As long as you're very, very careful and sensible." Mom and Dad had discussed this with them when they'd first booked the cottage. It was in a conservation area, where there were no roads—just a little track that led up to the cottage.

Alex and Becky nodded. They would be super-careful. They lived in a busy town, close to a main road that they had to cross in order to get anywhere, so Mom and Dad weren't happy about letting them take Cooper out on their own at home. That was why they had looked for a vacation home situated in a quiet place. Beachview Cottage wasn't far from a pretty seaside town called Salt Point, but it was all on its own on a cliff, surrounded by footpaths. It was going to be wonderful.

"I'm going to start packing when we get home," Becky said dreamily. "We'll have to remember to pack all of Cooper's things, too. I wonder if there's a pet store in Salt Point."

Alex smirked. "So you can buy him another fancy collar?" Then he rolled out of the way as Becky aimed a smack at him.

Cooper gave a little warning bark.

He didn't like it when they argued. He didn't understand that they were just teasing each other, even though Becky had tried telling him it was just what twins did. It seemed to Cooper that they were really angry with each other. He looked from Becky to Alex and back again, his eyes worried, and whined sadly.

"Sorry, Cooper." Becky wriggled over to him, and rubbed his ears and scratched his silky spaniel forehead. "It's okay. We were just playing."

Cooper flopped down, head on paws, with a small sigh of relief. His eyes were closing, and within seconds, he was asleep in the sun.

Chapter Three
An Ocean Vacation

"I wish Cooper could come in the back seat with us," said Becky as she gently placed the puppy in his travel crate in the back of the SUV. She caught Dad's eye and sighed. "Oh, it's all right, Dad. I know he can't. But it's just such a long trip! He's going to be miserable stuck in that crate. And it would be so nice to have him to cuddle on the way."

Dad shook his head. "Until he starts jumping around and being silly, and distracting me and Mom when we're driving. Don't worry. We'll stop at a rest area when we're halfway there, and we'll get Cooper out and you can take him to stretch his legs. He'll probably go to sleep, now that we've put his favorite blanket in the crate for him."

"I hope so," Becky said, patting Cooper gently and rubbing his ears before she closed the door of the crate. "See you soon, sweetheart."

"You get in, Becky. I'll go and see what's keeping your mom and Alex."

But Alex was already stomping down the path, lugging his backpack and looking grumpy. Mom followed along behind, shaking her head.

"He'd repacked everything!" she told Dad. "And taken out half the clothes! It's a good thing I checked. He had a skateboard in there instead!"

Dad blinked. "But I packed his skateboard—it's next to Cooper's travel crate. I'm sure I put it there."

Mom rolled her eyes. "Apparently he needs two."

"Wow. Oh, wow…," Becky breathed. She was standing in front of the cottage, with Cooper in her arms, staring out at the sea. He hadn't minded the car ride that much—he'd slept most of the time, like she had hoped. But he was definitely glad to be out of his crate.

They'd just arrived, and Becky and Alex had burst out of the car with Cooper to take a look around.

"It's beautiful," Becky whispered.

The sun was shining, and it had turned the water to silver, as though a sparkling pathway was stretched across the sea, calling them down to the beach.

"It really is right next to the sea," Alex said, grinning. He turned around to look at the cottage behind them, a small, white building, very low to the ground, as if it were trying to hide from the winds that swept across the cliff top. "And there's the path down to the beach —look!" He pointed to a little path, half natural, but with steps carved into it here and there to make the steep descent to the sand easier.

"Can we go down…?" Becky started to say, but Mom was waving to them.

"Come and help unpack. It won't take long, and then we can all head to the beach."

Becky sighed and headed back to the car to get her backpack. Cooper made a little whining noise, twisting in her arms to look at the glittering water. He wanted to go closer. He'd never seen anything like it before. Becky hugged him tightly. "I know, Cooper. I want to go and play down there, too. Soon, I promise."

She dashed inside, chasing after Alex, who was already stomping up the stairs. He flung open the bedroom door that Mom had pointed out and yelled, "I get the top bunk!"

"Hey, no fair!" Becky moaned from the doorway. Cooper wriggled out of her arms and went to explore. "Why do you get the top one? Can't we switch halfway through the vacation?"

Alex climbed up the ladder to throw his bag on the bed and stared down at her smugly. "Nope. I called it. Sorry, Becks."

Becky stamped her foot angrily, and Cooper, who was sniffing around under the bunk bed, backed farther underneath it, tucking his tail between his legs. They were fighting again. He hated it when they did that. Quietly, he sneaked along under the bed, heading for the bedroom door. Then he bolted out as Becky snapped at Alex, and stood shivering on the landing. He wanted to get away from the loud, scary voices.

Becky and Alex's mom had been looking around, checking out the different rooms and starting to put things away. She'd opened the door of the large cupboard at the top of the stairs, thinking to herself how useful it would be for hanging wet beach towels. Then she'd closed it again, but she didn't see that it had swung open a little as she walked away, and now Cooper nosed his way inside. It was warm and dark and safe next to the hot water tank, and no one was shouting in here. He curled up on an old towel that the last family must have left behind, and waited for his heart to stop thumping anxiously.

Back in the bedroom, Becky suddenly stopped arguing, and smiled as a thought occurred to her. "All right. You can have the top bunk. I don't mind."

"What?" Alex glared at her suspiciously. "For the entire vacation?"

Becky smiled even wider. "Yes. The entire vacation."

Alex nodded slowly. "Okay."

Becky sat down on the bottom bunk and patted it happily. "Cooper won't be able to get up the ladder, you know. So I get him on my bed for the entire time."

At home Cooper slept on either Becky's bed or Alex's, depending on how he felt. Sometimes he switched beds in the middle of the night, but he was usually curled up on Becky's toes when she woke up in the morning.

Alex scowled. "Hey, that's not fair…."

"You wanted the top bunk," Becky sang triumphantly. "Now you've got it!"

Alex slumped down next to her. "Humph. Cheater!"

"Nope, just more clever than you. Hey, where is Cooper?" Becky sat up, looking around worriedly. "He was exploring a minute ago. Oh, no—he hates when we fight."

Alex jumped up from the bed. "What if he ran outside? He doesn't have a clue where he's going around here."

They raced out of the bedroom, calling worriedly. "Cooper! Here, Cooper! Where are you, boy?"

"Did you lose him?" Mom popped her head out of her bedroom, looking anxious. "Oh, you two! I heard you fighting. Did you upset him?"

Dad came up the stairs. "I've been unloading the car and I haven't seen him come out the door. He must be in the cottage somewhere. Both of you really need to behave better around him. It's part of being proper dog owners—you have to be careful not to frighten your puppy."

"Sorry, Dad," Alex and Becky muttered, both looking guilty.

"He couldn't have gone far," said Dad. "Come on. I'll check downstairs and you two take another look up here."

"Maybe he's under the bed!" Alex dashed back into their room.

Becky looked along the landing, wondering where she would hide if she were a frightened little puppy. Somewhere dark and cozy, probably. Under the bed was a good idea…. Then she spotted the cupboard door, still slightly open, and padded quietly over to it. She swung the door open gently and crouched down to peer inside.

Cooper stared back at Becky, his eyes round and watchful, and thumped his tail slowly on the towel.

"Hey, Cooper…," Becky whispered sadly, looking at his worried little face. "We scared you, didn't we? Come on out, sweetie. We won't fight anymore."

Alex appeared behind her, and Becky glanced up warningly, her finger to her lips. Alex nodded. "It's okay, Cooper," he whispered. "We'll be nice."

Cooper stood up and nosed at Becky's hands lovingly. She picked him up, and Alex petted his ears gently.

"I'm really sorry, Cooper. Alex, we can't fight while we're here, okay?"

Becky looked at him seriously. "Or we have to try not to, anyway. We can't risk upsetting Cooper and having him run off in a strange place."

Alex nodded. "Vacation truce." He grinned. "Mom and Dad will be happy. Their quietest vacation ever!"

After the world's speediest lunch— Alex and Becky both claimed they weren't hungry, but Mom didn't believe them—they finally got to go down to the beach to explore with Cooper. It was amazing. Because the beach wasn't really close to the town, there was hardly anybody there—just one family building a sand castle, and a group of older boys swimming at one end.

"There's a bigger beach just a little farther along the coast down at Salt Point, with an ice-cream shop and a pier," Mom explained. "But you aren't allowed to take dogs onto Salt Point Beach in the summer."

"I don't mind." Becky gazed at the brown sand, which was striped with pebbles and framed by the tall, reddish-brown cliffs. "It's beautiful here. Just us and the ocean. Do you think we could let Cooper off the leash? He'd have to go all the way back up the path to get lost."

Dad nodded. "As long as we keep an eye on him."

Cooper barked excitedly as Becky

unclipped his leash. He wasn't used to being allowed to run off wherever he liked, and at first he simply raced up and down the sand, barking and jumping and chasing his tail.

Then he spotted an interesting pile of rather smelly seaweed that had been washed up onto the beach by the tide. Becky could see a line of it, all the way along the sand—seaweed, and shells, and even a piece of beautiful emerald green sea glass that she slipped into her pocket as a souvenir.

Alex was already splashing around in

the ocean, but Becky decided she needed some more time in the sun before taking a dip in the chilly water. She wondered if it might be too cold for Cooper, too. But Sam, their obedience class teacher, had told them that spaniels usually love water.

Cooper started to dig furiously, loving the way the sand spurted up between his paws. It was much quicker to dig here than in the flower beds at home. But it did go everywhere. He stopped mid-hole to shake the sand out of his whiskers, and let out an enormous sneeze. Next he dragged a big pile of seaweed into his hole and covered it back over, scooting the sand back through his paws. Then he sat down on it happily, looking very proud of himself.

Becky watched him, laughing. "Should we go and see the water now?" she asked him. "Look, Alex is paddling in it."

Cooper stood up and followed her down to the water's edge, where Alex was hopping in and out of the waves, whistling through his teeth at how cold it was.

Cooper watched interestedly, his tail wagging. He'd never seen so much water, and it moved! He backed away thoughtfully as the bubbly surf crept toward him, and then followed it back again, fascinated.

"Oh, look, Alex! He loves it!" Becky giggled.

The puppy crouched down, his paws stretched out in front of him, wondering if he could catch this stuff. This time, when the creamy water began to draw back from his paws, he jumped after it, splashing himself and Becky with freezing cold water.

Becky laughed, and Cooper shook himself in surprise. He hadn't expected that to happen. But he liked it!

When the next wave came, he didn't try to catch the water; he just jumped in and out of it, shaking his soaked ears and whining excitedly. Chasing the waves was almost as much fun as chasing squirrels!

Chapter Four
A Cliffside Walk

On that first afternoon of vacation, Becky and Alex had been so eager to get down to the beach that they'd hardly taken anything with them. But the next morning, the first real full day in Salt Point, they took everything: water toys, towels, shovels, snacks, blankets, and Alex's enormous inflatable alligator. They struggled down the path, laden with all they could possibly need, and Mom and Dad followed them with folding chairs and a picnic lunch.

It was another beautiful sunny day, and Mom insisted on covering them with sunscreen as soon as they'd set up a base camp next to a large rock. She looked doubtfully at Cooper. "I guess he'll be all right. But if he starts to look hot, you must bring him back over here so he can lie down in the shade of the rocks."

"Okay, but he'll probably just splash in the ocean like he did yesterday," Becky pointed out. "That'll keep him nice and cool."

Cooper was already running up and down the water's edge, barking excitedly at seagulls, who shrieked back angrily.

One of them settled down to float on the greenish water, not very far out, and glared at him.

Cooper splashed into the ocean, so it came halfway up his short legs, and barked a challenge. But the seagull only bobbed up and down and kept on staring. Cooper took a few more steps in, shivering a little as the water came up to his chest.

Becky had been sitting rubbing sunscreen onto her arms and watching Alex, who was kicking a ball around farther up the beach. But now she suddenly noticed that Cooper was in the water. She raced down to the edge of the ocean, but Dad was there already.

"It's okay, Becks. A lot of dogs are

good swimmers. We can't let him go out too far, but don't scare him now. We don't want him to think that the water is something to be afraid of."

Becky frowned. Actually, she thought maybe they did. What if Cooper got swept away by a big wave? And that seagull looked like it wanted puppy for breakfast. It was staring at Cooper with its tiny yellow eyes.

Cooper looked around, happy to see Becky so close, and then took another step forward. Strangely, though, his paws didn't seem to find any ground to step on, and all of a sudden he was swimming, doggy-paddling as though he'd been doing it forever. Rather surprised at himself, he paddled around in a little circle, almost forgetting about the seagull.

"He's swimming! He's swimming!" Becky yelled. "Cooper can swim! Dad, look!"

The seagull flapped its powerful wings and fluttered away with loud, frightened squawks, and Cooper barked at it.

"Sorry, Cooper!" Becky splashed into the water. "I forgot you were chasing him. You're such a clever boy! How did you learn to swim? Come on!" She dog-paddled along with him, even though she was in such shallow water that her knees kept hitting the sand. "Do you think he can swim a little farther out, Dad?" she called.

Dad shook his head. "Maybe not yet—he might get tired quickly, like he did with walks at first. Remember, he has never done it before. Just splash around in the shallow water with him."

Alex came running down the beach to join in, and they spent the next hour swimming out into the ocean and then back to the beach and letting the little waves carry them up onto the sand, while Cooper swam and splashed and barked delightedly around them.

They were worn out by lunchtime, so much so that Cooper went to sleep in the shade of the big rock after he'd eaten his dog biscuits and had a big drink of water. Alex and Becky lazed around reading while they digested their sandwiches— Mom said they had to wait for a while before going back in the water.

"It's been forever since lunch…," Alex moaned. "Can we go swimming again?"

"It's only been about 10 minutes!" Mom laughed, and Alex sighed.

"All right. I'm going to blow up my alligator." He lay down on the blanket and puffed fiercely, until the alligator was taller than he was. "Now can we go swimming?"

Mom looked at her watch. "Yes,

I suppose so. Oh, Cooper!"

Cooper had just woken up and found an enormous green thing next to Alex, which definitely hadn't been there when he went to sleep. He raced over and barked at it madly, running around and around it, kicking sand on everybody.

"Ugh! Stop him!" Mom coughed, and Alex snatched the alligator up above his head, while Becky grabbed Cooper.

"Cooper, stop! Shhh! It's not a real one, silly. It's for swimming. Come on, Alex, let's show him. The water will wash the sand off us, too." She carried the squirming puppy down to the water's edge, and Alex launched the alligator into the waves.

"We'll have to be careful that Cooper

doesn't pop it with his claws," he said, holding the alligator steady.

Becky leaped on board and lay down. "You can tow us," she suggested, holding onto the side. "Come on, Cooper." She held out an arm, expecting the puppy to swim toward it, but instead he splashed into the water, paddled out to her, then scrambled up onto her back.

"You're a raft!" Alex yelled, and Becky giggled, trying not to wriggle too much and tip Cooper off. His claws tickled.

They swam up and down, taking turns on the alligator, and then pulled it up onto the beach and lay there on the sand, letting the tiny waves wash over their toes.

The sun was so hot, even when they were half in the water, that Becky almost fell asleep. She was just wondering how it was that the water seemed as warm as a bath now, when it had been freezing when she first dipped her toes in that morning, when Alex suddenly sat up and yelled. "Look! The alligator!"

She turned over and sat up. "What's the matter?"

"I wasn't watching. The tide must have come in," Alex groaned. "The waves have taken it out. I'll have to go out and get it."

Becky stood up. "I can't even see it. Oh, no! Alex, you can't swim all the way out there."

The alligator was only a little green spot, about 100 feet from the shore, where they'd be out in water that was much too deep.

"Dad!" Alex called. But their dad still had all his clothes on, and even though he was heading over toward them, and Mom was standing on the blanket looking worried, neither of them looked like they were about to dive into the ocean.

"Dad, can I swim out and get the alligator?" Alex begged. But Dad shook his head.

"I'm really sorry, Alex. It's drifted too

far. You promised not to go into deep water, remember? Maybe someone in a boat will come by and pick it up for us."

Alex and Becky looked hopefully out over the water, but there were no boats around to go alligator-hunting, and the inflatable was bobbing farther and farther away.

Then Alex grabbed Becky's arm and pointed. A little golden head was suddenly bobbing through the dark-green water. Cooper could see the inflatable, and he knew that Alex wanted it back. He wasn't quite sure why Alex wasn't going to get it himself, but he knew he could help.

"Cooper, no!" Becky gasped. But Cooper was already way out into the water, swimming along happily.

"He's too far out," Becky said worriedly. "What if he gets caught in a current and he's swept right out to sea?"

Alex nodded. "Let's swim out as far as we can—then we can help him back."

They swam as fast as they could, to where their toes were just touching the bottom. Mom and Dad were watching. Although Becky and Alex had promised them not to go too far out, secretly Becky knew that if Cooper started sinking, she'd follow him right out into the deep water. And she was sure Alex would do the same.

But they didn't need to. Slowly but surely, the alligator was bobbing back toward them, Cooper's sharp teeth gripping the white tow rope.

"Great job, Cooper! You rescued my alligator!" Alex grabbed the rope, too, and Becky hugged Cooper, who snuggled wearily into her shoulder. It had been a long swim, and his legs were very tired. But he had done it! Becky and Alex were happy, he could tell.

"Becks, get on the alligator with him,

and I'll pull you along," Alex suggested.

Becky nodded and heaved herself up onto the inflatable, carefully keeping Cooper's claws away from the plastic. Alex towed them back in, with Becky proudly holding Cooper in front of her.

Mom and Dad were waiting for them on the beach, smiling with relief.

"I can't believe what a good swimmer he is!" Mom said, scratching Cooper's wet ears.

"He's a champion," Alex said proudly. "We would have lost my alligator for sure if it hadn't been for Cooper."

Becky turned over in bed and yawned, and then giggled as a damp nose was pressed into her ear. "Hello, Cooper! Is it time to get up?" She wriggled up in bed, and pulled open the curtains to look out the little window right next to the bunks.

"Oh!" Becky wrinkled her nose disappointedly. The sparkling blue water of the day before had disappeared. The sky was cloudy and the ocean had settled to a dull grayish brown—it didn't look like a day for sunbathing or swimming at all.

"Oh, well," Becky muttered. "It's okay, Cooper. Maybe we can go exploring along the cliffs instead."

She got out of bed and threw on jeans and a T-shirt. She could already hear Mom and Dad moving around downstairs, and she thought she could smell toast. Cooper would need to go out into the tiny yard behind the cottage to relieve himself, too.

"Wake up, Alex," she called, tickling the foot that was dangling down over the edge of the top bunk as she went past.

Alex growled something, but his comforter humped up as if he were at least partly awake.

"Let's go and explore the cliffs this morning," Becky suggested a few minutes later as she sat down at the table for breakfast. Cooper was already sitting hopefully by her foot, waiting for toast crusts.

But Alex shook his head grumpily. "No! I really want to go down to the beach at Salt Point. You said we could,

Dad! They've got rides on the pier there, and everything. I was talking to those boys we saw on the beach on our first day, and they said it's awesome there."

Becky frowned. "But we wouldn't be able to take Cooper! Salt Point Beach doesn't allow dogs in the summer, Mom said."

"Anyway, it's not very nice weather today," Mom put in. "It feels more like a day for walking along the cliffs than going to the beach. We'll do that another day, Alex."

Alex muttered something under his breath, but Mom managed to distract him by passing him chocolate-hazelnut spread for his toast, which was a vacation treat.

After breakfast, they set off along the path that led from the cottage, winding through the shrubs and prickly bushes along the top of the cliff. Cooper danced ahead, tugging on his extending leash, and winding himself in and out of the shrubs as he investigated all the interesting sandy holes.

"Let's take him off the leash," Becky suggested after she'd unwound him from the bushes for the third time. "There's no one else up here."

But before Dad could answer, Cooper uttered a sharp little woof and looked around at her excitedly.

"What is it?" she asked, and then she gasped. "Oh, look! A rabbit!"

A small sandy-brown rabbit was peering back at them from the middle of a bush. It looked terrified.

"Poor thing!" Becky whispered. "It's so scared. Cooper, you can't chase it!" But Cooper was already darting forward, the cord of his leash getting longer as he raced after the rabbit, which turned tail and dived down a nearby hole.

"Oh, Cooper!" Becky tried to pull him back, but he had his nose in the hole and was barking frantically. He'd been within a few feet of a real rabbit, and now it had disappeared! He could still smell it, but he couldn't see it. He dug and scratched, but he couldn't get any farther in because the hole was too narrow. Eventually he gave up and slunk sadly back to Becky. For some reason she seemed angry, but he had no idea why.

"That rabbit was terrified! You shouldn't have chased it, Cooper!"

Alex snorted. "Come on, Becky! He's a dog! That's what dogs do! Spaniels were bred for hunting."

"But Cooper's a pet, not a hunting dog! What if he starts to like hunting things and chasing cats?" Becky snapped back. "Then he'd be in real trouble. Imagine Mrs. Winter next door if he chased Jewel!" Jewel was Mrs. Winter's enormous fluffy Persian cat. Becky sighed, looking down at Cooper, who was watching her with confused eyes and slowly wagging his tail. "Oh, it isn't your fault, Cooper. I'm not really angry. It was such a cute rabbit, that's all."

"Anyway, that answers the question about letting him off the leash," Dad pointed out. "Have you noticed how close we are to the edge of the cliff?" He crouched down, pushing aside some clumps of yellow flowers to show the animal holes dotted around between them—and the little sandy slope trailing down to the edge. "If a rabbit popped up in front of Cooper and ducked into one of those holes over there, he'd be over the side of the cliff before you could even call his name."

Becky shuddered. "I suppose you're right. Okay, we'll keep the leash on."

Cooper wandered on, sniffing hopefully for more rabbits, but they all seemed to have hidden themselves away. For the rest of the walk he had to make do with leaping at the butterflies, a lot of tiny little blue ones, which kept flying around his nose.

Chapter Five
Trouble!

The next couple of days were sunny again, and the family spent them on the beach. Cooper and the children were in and out of the ocean most of the time because it was so hot out and the only way to cool down.

The group of boys who'd been on the beach before were back again on Wednesday, playing soccer, and Alex watched them hopefully for a while, before the ball happened to come past him. He kicked it back expertly, and they invited him to come and join in. Becky didn't mind being left on her own with Cooper, Mom, and Dad. It was much too hot for soccer, and it was fun reading her book with Cooper snoozing next to her in the sun.

"Mom! Dad! Josh and Liam's dad is taking them to Salt Point Beach this afternoon, and they asked if I want to go, too. Can I? And can I take my vacation money for the rides?"

Dad got up and went to talk to Josh and Liam's dad.

"What about you, Becky?" Mom asked. "Dad and I could take you if you wanted to go over to Salt Point."

Becky looked thoughtful, but then she shook her head. "Actually, I'd rather stay here, Mom." She didn't like going on rides, and she was really enjoying spending her vacation time with Cooper.

Alex went off with the other boys after lunch, and Becky set off on a long walk up the beach with Cooper. She hunted for shells and sea glass, and Cooper found a dead fish. He was upset when Becky threw it back into the ocean and wouldn't let him fetch it. It had smelled delicious.

On Thursday morning, Becky and Alex were hoping to go to the beach again, but Mom pointed out that they really needed to go grocery shopping.

"Do we have to come?" Alex groaned.

"Well, you can't go to the beach by yourselves." Mom shook her head. "Dad or I need to be there if you're going in the ocean."

"We could just stay out of the water," Becky suggested. But then she shook her head. "Actually, I don't see how we'd explain to Cooper that he couldn't go swimming. It probably isn't a very good idea."

"What about a walk, though?" Alex asked. "You did say before we came that we'd be allowed to go out on our own and we haven't yet."

"Yes, and Cooper really needs a walk, too," Becky added, exchanging an excited glance with Alex.

Mom and Dad looked thoughtfully at each other. "I suppose you could,"

Dad said slowly. "We won't be more than a couple of hours. As long as you take one of our cell phones, and you promise not to do anything silly."

"Great!" Alex cheered, and Becky reached under the table to pet Cooper. She could hardly wait for them to take their puppy out on their own for the first time ever.

After breakfast, Alex tucked Mom's cell phone safely away in the pocket of his shorts, and he and Becky filled a little bag with sunscreen, snacks, dog treats, water, and Cooper's special folding dog bowl. It was so hot that he was going to need a drink for sure.

It felt like a real adventure, setting off on their own with Cooper, and they were determined to make it a really long walk.

"We could go all the way around the top of the bay," Alex suggested as he hurried along, holding Cooper's leash. "The cliffs over toward Salt Point looked really interesting from the beach. There might be caves and things in them. And we could look for fossils!"

But by the time they'd fought their way through the prickly bushes as far as they'd gone on that first cliff-top walk, Becky and Alex were so hot that they decided to stop for a break. Becky filled up Cooper's bowl, and he drank greedily. He'd walked more than twice as far as Becky and Alex, as he kept running backward and forward. He lay there in the cool shade of the ferns, occasionally snapping lazily at dragonflies as they zipped past. Alex sat on the leash, just in case, but it didn't look as though Cooper wanted to run off anyway.

"My turn to take Cooper now," Becky said as she packed his bowl away in the bag and got up. "You can carry the bag."

Alex scowled. "Why should you always get to hold his leash? I'm taking him for this walk. You had him all yesterday afternoon!"

"What? For the whole walk? That isn't fair!" Becky yelled. "I only had him yesterday because you wanted to go to Salt Point! You didn't care about Cooper then, did you?"

Cooper looked up and whined worriedly.

"Oh, it's okay, Cooper … don't be scared." She turned to her brother. "Now look!" she hissed. "You're upsetting Cooper!"

"I'm not the one arguing!" Alex spat back in a whisper. "Just let me hold him! This walk was my idea, remember?"

"No! It's my turn!"

Cooper whined again, but they weren't listening. He backed away, the leash pulling out behind him, and his tail held close against his legs. He didn't want to be near them when they shouted at each other. It scared him. He'd go and find somewhere safe to hide until they stopped, he decided. He headed a little farther down the path. His extending leash was very long, so he could get a good distance away from the loud voices. The delicious smells in the undergrowth soon distracted him from the squabble he'd left behind, and he nosed around the bushes, sure he could smell a rabbit somewhere near.

There was no rabbit to be found, but there was a huge butterfly—a brown one that swooped temptingly right in front of his nose. He barked happily and chased after it as it fluttered away. He'd never actually caught one before, but he was so close to this one that surely it couldn't get away. He ran on, barking excitedly and snapping at the butterfly, sure that Becky and Alex would be happy if he finally caught one.

Just then, Becky grabbed at the leash, yanking it away from Alex. As she reached for the leash's bulky plastic handle, she lost her balance, and the handle slipped out of her hands. She dived after it, and so did Alex—but it was too late. They watched the leash sliding away as Cooper raced after the butterfly.

"Cooper!" Becky yelled, scrambling after the leash as it disappeared down the path. She could just see Cooper's golden tail, wagging excitedly as he chased after something up ahead. Becky took off after him—just as Cooper made one last desperate lunge after the butterfly, and tumbled over the side of the cliff, his leash bouncing uselessly behind him.

Chapter Six
A Desperate Situation

Cooper scratched and scrambled down the steep slope, trying frantically to stop himself by clawing at the reddish side of the cliff as he fell. Sharper rocks were sticking out of the sandy earth every so often, and he whimpered as one of his paws caught against a particularly large stone.

At last, he landed on a tiny ledge, about

15 feet down the side of the cliff. He sat there cowering and shivering, holding up his bleeding paw and howling with fright. What had happened? All he had done was follow the butterfly! It had disappeared, and the path had gone with it. Where were Becky and Alex? He wanted Becky to take care of his paw and pet him, and get him out of this horrible place.

"Cooper!" Becky screamed, racing along the path to the spot where he'd disappeared, with Alex dashing after her. "Where is he?" She flung herself down at the edge of the cliff to peer over and suddenly felt sick, her head swimming as she looked at the ocean so far below. When they were on the beach, the cliffs had looked so pretty, pinkish-red with sandy streaks, but now they seemed menacing and sinister, and very, very tall. The ocean was right in at the bottom now, frothing and rushing around in clouds of bubbles and foam. Even though Cooper was a good swimmer, she didn't see how he could have survived such a terrible fall.

"Can you see him?" Alex asked, his voice quiet and miserable. Becky shook her head. "No. He must be—under the water…," she said, her voice choked with tears.

But then there was a pitiful wail from below, and Becky gasped. "Alex, look! He's there, he's there!"

She pointed to a tiny ledge below, where a clump of bushes and straggly bits of grass had somehow managed to find some soil to grow in. It was just above the tumble of rocks rising out of the water at the base of the cliff. Sitting there, staring up at them mournfully, was Cooper.

"Cooper, stay! We'll come and get you—or—or something…." Becky's voice trailed away.

"He's all right. He's actually okay…," Alex whispered, gripping tightly onto two handfuls of grass, and leaning as far as he possibly could without going over, too. "I can't believe he managed to fall down there and still be okay."

Becky gulped, and tears welled up in her eyes. Alex put his arm around her. They were both shaking.

"He's moving, definitely. But I think he hurt his paw. It's so hard to see," Becky muttered. "I shouldn't have tried to grab the leash from you. I'm really sorry." She stared down at Cooper. "How are we going to get him back? It's such a long way down to that ledge."

Alex looked worriedly at Cooper. "I think you're right. He's holding his paw in a funny way. There's no way he'll be able to climb back up here! I wonder if I can scramble down to him."

Becky grabbed his arm tightly. "Are you crazy? Look how steep it is! You'll fall!"

Alex shook his head. "Look over there—it's almost like a path, down to where Cooper is."

"Well, I can't see it," Becky said stubbornly. She could kind of see, but it didn't look like much of a path, and she was scared that Alex was going to fall, too. It was only a very thin ledge, weaving its way toward the bigger ledge that Cooper was on.

Cooper howled again, and Becky called down to him. "It's okay, Cooper! Don't be scared!" She looked back up at Alex. "Are you sure you can get down there?"

Alex shrugged. "No. But I want to try. It was my fault, too, that this happened." He went over to the little break in the cliff edge where the tiny path started and gazed at it, chewing his lip. "I'll sit and wriggle along, I think." He edged himself down, very slowly, and Becky watched, her heart racing.

Cooper stared up from his ledge and wagged his tail hopefully. Alex was coming to get him! He stood up, wincing as he tried to put his hurt paw on the ground, and then he had to flop down again. There was definitely something wrong with his leg.

He could see Becky, too, just her face, peering over the edge of the cliff, so very far away. Cooper let out a miserable howl. He wanted to be back up there with her!

"It's okay, Cooper, shhh!" Becky called out, trying to make her voice calm and comforting. Their obedience class teacher had said that voices were really important. If she sounded scared and upset, Cooper would be scared, too. She had to keep him calm. He always listened best to her in obedience classes; Alex got him too excited. Now it was more important than ever to keep Cooper calm. The little ledge he was on was so narrow. If Cooper got frightened and scrambled around, he could easily fall into that treacherous-looking ocean. And with an injured leg, he might not be able to swim.

Becky watched nervously as Alex inched down the path toward Cooper. He was going as slowly and carefully as he could, but the path was very steep.

Suddenly, Becky gasped as Alex's feet went out from under him, and he slid down in a rattle of sand and tiny pebbles. She caught her breath, jamming her knuckles into her mouth to keep herself from crying out.

Alex yelled in panic, and grabbed onto a bush, hanging on even though it scratched his hands.

"Alex!" Becky called down. "Are you all right? You have to come back up. It isn't safe. We'll call Mom and Dad."

Alex nodded. "I'm sorry, Cooper," he called down sadly. "We're going to get help, I promise." He dragged himself back up, going hand over hand and holding onto the scrubby plants that lined the path.

Becky grabbed him as soon as he

got near the top. "We should have called Mom and Dad right away. Are you okay?"

Alex nodded. "Just a little scratched." He showed her his hands. "But it was really scary. Poor Cooper. He fell a lot farther down than I did." He reached into his pocket for the phone and pressed the menu button to bring the screen on.

Nothing happened.

Becky and Alex stared at it in horror. "Try again!" Becky said hopefully, but the phone remained stubbornly lifeless.

"I must have hit it on something when I fell. Mom's going to be furious...," Alex muttered.

"That doesn't matter now. What are we going to do?" Becky looked around, hoping that there might be somebody else walking along the cliff top. But they were all alone.

"I'll have to run back down to the road—there's a pay phone, isn't there? I have some money left from yesterday. You stay here with Cooper. You really need to keep him calm; you're good at that. We don't want him trying to climb up and falling even farther." Alex frowned. "Becks, I can't remember Dad's cell phone number, can you?"

Becky shook her head miserably. "No. But it doesn't matter," she added suddenly. "Dad wouldn't be able to get down the cliff, either. It's just too dangerous. You'll have to call the Coast Guard."

Alex nodded nervously. He'd never made an emergency call before—but this was definitely an emergency.

Chapter Seven
Rescued!

Becky watched as Alex raced off down the path, leaving her all alone on the cliff top, with only the seagulls shrieking around her. Then she leaned over the edge again, digging her toes into the sandy earth so that she felt safer wriggling out a couple more inches over the edge. She felt dizzy staring down at the water, which seemed to be crashing

against the cliffs harder and harder
every time she looked.

Cooper was curled up in a little ball
now, with his nose tucked in next to
his tail. He looked so tiny that Becky
wanted to cry.

"Cooper!" she called down to him.

Cooper glanced up and barked
delightedly. He'd thought that Becky
and Alex had left him here alone. He
had no idea how he was ever going
to get back up the cliff. He'd looked
down at the water on the rocks below,
and wondered if he should jump in and
swim until he found the beach, but the
water looked very different from the
ocean he'd swum in before. His little
ledge was just above the waves, which
kept rolling in and sending cold spray

up at him. And the rocks looked slippery and scary. His paw hurt, too, and he wasn't sure he'd even be able to swim. He'd pressed himself back against the cliff wall instead and curled into a ball, whimpering sadly to himself, wishing someone were there to help him. And then he'd heard Becky!

Maybe he could climb back up to her! The ledge was very thin, and it trailed off into a tiny little path that went winding up the cliff. Becky wasn't really all that far away, Cooper thought, staring up at her white and anxious face. He limped along to where the ledge got smaller and looked thoughtfully up at the path. It was very narrow. He started off up it, squeezing himself as close as he could to the side of the cliff and feeling the sand trickle down into his fur.

"Cooper, stay!" Becky was calling to him. She sounded worried—angry, almost. He was only trying to reach her. Why was she angry? But he knew what "stay" meant from his obedience classes. He had to do as he was told, even though he really didn't want to. He sat down on the path, his ears drooping, feeling confused.

"It's okay, Cooper. I'm sorry. I'm so sorry...." Up on the cliff, Becky took a deep breath and tried not to feel scared. It just felt like Alex had been gone for such a long time. Every time she looked down, Cooper's little ledge seemed to have grown even narrower, and the ocean wilder. And if the tide came up much more, the ledge would be underwater! She tried to remember when high tide had been the day before, but her mind felt foggy.

"Good boy, Cooper. Stay! What a good boy! A lot of biscuits soon. Stay! That's it." *Just don't move, Cooper, please!* she added silently to herself.

"Becky! Becky!"

Cooper looked up, his tail wagging. Alex had come back, too! He tried to bark happily to show Alex he was happy to see him, but jumping around hurt his paw, and his balance seemed all wrong. He slid backward, scratching and yelping, and Becky and Alex's faces appeared over the edge of the cliff, both looking horrified.

"Cooper, stay still!" Alex yelled. His voice was sharp and fierce, and it made Cooper feel scared. He skittered around on the ledge anxiously.

"Down, Cooper! Down! Stay!" That was Becky again. She didn't sound scared like Alex, but she sounded very firm. Not angry, but he could tell that he had to do as she said or she would be upset. Cooper lay down flat on the ledge, feeling the cold water splash over his back. He wanted to get away. He hated it down here! He howled and howled. But he kept still.

Up above Cooper on the cliff, Alex explained to Becky what was happening. "I got to the pay phone and called the Coast Guard. But I didn't know exactly where we were on the cliffs; I hope I told them the right place. I said it was just up from Beachview Cottage."

"Are they sending someone?" Becky asked anxiously.

"Yes, they said the boat will come out from the Salt Point harbor, and it won't take long at all. The lady on the phone said it might even get here before I did."

"Did she say to do anything else?"

Alex shook his head. "Just to come back and try to keep Cooper calm, and you're doing a great job of that. And we should watch for the boat and wave in case they can't see Cooper." He propped himself up on his elbows, staring out at the water. "That's not a Coast Guard boat, is it?" he asked, pointing to a small boat, far out on the waves.

Becky shook her head. "No, I think that's the ferry boat from Salt Point. Anyway, the Coast Guard boat won't be that far out, I bet. It'll come around the edge of the bay." She frowned down at Cooper on his ledge, and the nasty-looking rocks below him. "How are they going to get to him, Alex? They won't be able to get a boat close up to those rocks, will they?"

"If it's the inflatable, they will. I saw it in the boat shed when I went to Salt Point Beach yesterday. It's made for going in and out of the rocks around the coast. Look, there are people on the cliffs—maybe they saw it being launched. Josh and Liam said people always go up there to watch when the Coast Guard boat goes out."

Becky nodded, watching the little crowd of people gathering along the cliffs above the beach. She could see they were chatting and pointing at Cooper. If it had been another dog, she would have been interested, too. Now it only made her feel sick.

"Becks, look! I can see it coming!"

The Coast Guard boat was roaring

around the far edge of the cliffs in a cloud of spray, and bouncing over the water toward them. It was small, and there were only three crew members, but it was very, very fast.

"I wish Mom and Dad were here," Becky said worriedly as the little gray boat shot toward them. "Maybe they saw the boat being launched from Salt Point when they were shopping. Do you think they'd come back to see what was going on?"

"Maybe. They might even be in that crowd over there." Alex hugged her.

The boat was getting closer now, and they could see the Coast Guard men waving to them. They waved back and pointed down to Cooper.

Cooper could see the boat coming, too. It was very loud, and he didn't like it at all. He barked at it, wishing it would go away.

"Shhh, Cooper, it's okay!" Becky called down. "I think he's scared of the boat. Cooper, stay!"

The Coast Guard boat had stopped by the rocks, and one of the men was climbing out. Becky held her breath anxiously. It looked so slippery.

"Hello up there!" the man called to Alex and Becky. "He looks pretty scared. Can you get him to stay? I don't want to scare him into jumping."

Becky nodded. "Cooper, stay there! Stay!"

Cooper stared wide-eyed at the man in the bright orange suit, with his huge life jacket and orange helmet. He looked like some sort of strange creature, and he'd arrived in that huge noisy thing that was still grumbling and snorting below him. Cooper gave a loud series of barks, trying to sound big and scary. But the man didn't go away. He slowly climbed closer instead. Cooper looked around, desperate for a way to escape. There was only the little narrow path where he'd already slipped. But he didn't have a choice. He started to back away up it, still barking at the strange man.

"Cooper, no!" It was Becky, calling him from up above. "Stay! Cooper, stay!"

Cooper knew he should do as he was told, but he didn't want to stay! The strange man was coming after him!

"Stay, Cooper!" It was Becky's firmest voice. If he did as he was told, he might get dog treats—he knew Becky had them in her bag. And he was very hungry. The man was coming closer. Cooper stayed still and looked imploringly up at Becky. Did he really have to stay?

"Yes, good boy, Cooper! Stay!" Becky sounded pleased with him.

The man was almost at his ledge now, and Cooper wanted to growl at him. He didn't look nice at all with that big orange helmet on. But he kept quiet. He was sure Becky wouldn't want him to growl.

"You're a good dog, aren't you?" the man called as he climbed onto the ledge. The man's voice was actually nice, and

Cooper stopped shivering. "Look what I have." The man held out a piece of dog biscuit, and Cooper gulped it down gratefully. Maybe he wasn't so bad after all, even if he did look scary. "Want some more?" The man reached out and picked him up, and gave him a full biscuit this time. "Aren't you adorable? Come on." And he started back over the rocks to the boat, with Cooper tucked tightly under one arm.

Up on the top of the cliff, Becky hugged Alex tightly. "They've got him, they've got him! Cooper's really going to be okay!"

Chapter Eight
Safe at Last

Alex hugged Becky back, laughing, and then turned back to peer over the edge. "Hey, wait! They're calling to us!"

"We'll take him around to the small beach in the boat!" one of the men shouted up to Alex and Becky. "We'll meet you there, okay? Are you both all right? Not hurt, are you?"

"We're fine! Thank you!" Alex yelled

back, and Becky called, "Good boy, Cooper!" They raced back along the top of the cliff as fast as they could, heading for the path down to the beach just in front of the cottage.

"I can see our car parked behind the cottage!" Alex yelled to Becky. "Mom and Dad are probably down on the beach. We would have run into them on the path if they'd come after us. They must have seen the boat and gone to watch."

They scrambled down the path and ran across the sand to the little group of people who had gathered to watch the Coast Guard boat pull in. It beached with a soft crunch of sand, and one of the men jumped over the side into the water, which only came halfway up his big orange boots. Another of the men handed Cooper over the side to the first man, and Becky ran into the water to take him, even though she had her sneakers on.

Cooper was squeaking with delight at seeing Becky and Alex, and he wriggled madly, trying to get out of the man's arms to reach her.

"He's a wonderful little dog," the man told her as he handed Cooper over. "Take good care of him, okay? Don't let him go near the edge of any more cliffs."

"I won't," Becky said. "It was my fault that he fell. We'll be more careful, I promise." She laughed as Cooper licked her all over, and then licked Alex's face, too.

"You were right to call 911, though," the man told them. "Don't ever go climbing down those cliffs yourselves."

Alex shuddered. "We won't."

"Becky! Alex!"

Mom and Dad were making their way through the small crowd, looking horrified.

"What on earth happened?" Mom demanded.

"We're sorry, Mom…," they muttered.

"There was an accident," Becky added.

"Cooper fell over the edge of the cliff."

"That cliff?" Dad gazed up at it, his face pale. "But we agreed you'd keep him on the leash up there." Dad looked from Becky to Alex. He seemed really disappointed.

"They did the right thing," the Coast Guard officer told Mom and Dad. "They called 911 and got us out to help."

Mom nodded. "Thank you so much."

Becky caught her arm. "Mom, can we explain later, please? Cooper hurt his leg when he fell; we have to take him to a vet."

"There's a vet on the main street in town , just down from the supermarket," the Coast Guard officer told them. "Good luck. I hope it's nothing too serious." And he splashed back to the boat, with everyone waving and cheering, and they sped away.

Cooper yawned sleepily and licked at the bandage on his paw. It was itchy, and he was sure if he nibbled it carefully, he could pull it off.

"Hey, don't do that, Cooper." Becky sat down beside him and tickled him under the chin. "You know if you keep chewing it, you'll have to wear that horrible collar thing, and you wouldn't like that. The vet says the bandage has to stay on for at least a week."

"He was so lucky not to break anything," Mom said. "Only four stitches, and some pulled muscles. It could have been so much worse." Mom's face was serious. After they'd gotten back from the vet the day before, she and Dad had made Becky and Alex sit down and tell them exactly what had happened up on the cliff path. They'd felt awful as they explained that it was all their fault that Cooper had fallen and gotten hurt. Then Mom and Dad had told them how disappointed they were.

Becky shivered. "I know," she said. "I don't want to go along the cliff-top path ever again."

"Me, neither," Alex agreed, munching on a slice of toast covered with chocolate-hazelnut spread.

"It's a shame not to go out, though," said Mom, getting up to look at the weather from the window. "It's such a beautiful day. You two could go down to the beach with Dad, if you'd like. I can stay and watch Cooper."

Becky shook her head and glanced at Alex to see that he was doing the same. "I'd rather stay here and be with Cooper," she explained. "Yesterday was so scary. I just want to be with him for a little while." She rubbed his ears lovingly, and Cooper yawned and nudged her with his little damp nose.

Alex came over and slipped Cooper a dog treat. Cooper gulped it down happily. Everyone was being so nice to him!

Dad nodded. "Well, we still have three more days of vacation left. Cooper might be all right to go down to the beach tomorrow if we're careful. And it's good just having a quiet day, anyway."

There was a loud knock at the door, and Alex burst out laughing.

Dad sighed. "What did I say that for?" He got up and went to the front door, coming back with a dark-haired woman with a big camera hanging around her neck. "It seems you're famous, you two," Dad said, smiling. "This is Melissa from the local paper. She heard all about yesterday's adventure and wants a photo of you and Cooper."

"It's such a heartwarming story," the reporter explained. "And you called the Coast Guard yourselves? That was really good thinking."

Alex grinned proudly. "That was me. But it was actually Becky who kept Cooper safe the entire time that he was on the ledge. She was wonderful at getting him to stay."

Becky smiled. "But it was our fault that Cooper fell," she added sadly. "We were arguing over who got to hold his leash and we dropped it, and he ran off and slipped over the edge of the cliff."

Melissa smiled. "I don't think I'll put that in. These things happen, don't they? I used to fight with my brother all the time. We'll just remind people to be extra careful when they're walking up on the cliffs." Cooper jumped down from the sofa and went to give Melissa a curious sniff. "And this is Cooper?" She patted Cooper, and he licked her fingers, making her laugh.

"He's a real sweetheart. And it sounds like he was lucky, too!"

Cooper barked happily. The lady was right—he was lucky. He knew that!

Becky beamed as they posed with Cooper for the newspaper photo—she and Alex on either side of their beautiful puppy. She knew he'd had an amazing escape. Becky rubbed Cooper's silky golden ears and smiled at the camera.

Right now, she felt like the luckiest girl ever.

The
Tiniest
Puppy

Contents

For William and Robin

Chapter One
An Exciting Time

"Baylee looks so big!" Lauren peered under the kitchen table at the family's beagle. They had adopted Baylee from the rescue center last year, and she had settled in with the family quite nicely. She was sitting at their feet, panting and looking uncomfortable. Her tummy was huge, and the expression on her face was a little grumpy.

Dad checked under the table, too. "Well, she's due to have the puppies any day now. I'll take her temperature later to see if it has gone down."

Lauren nodded. They had been taking Baylee's temperature every day for the last couple of weeks. The vet, Mike, had told them it was the best way to tell when the puppies were about to come.

Baylee padded heavily out from under the table and wandered over to her cushion. She took hold of the edge in her teeth—it was a big, soft cushion, made of red fabric—and tugged it closer to the radiator. Then she nudged it with her nose, this way and that, as though she couldn't get it quite how she wanted it.

Lauren watched her hopefully. "Does that look like nesting to you?" she asked.

"I don't know. It might be...," her mom said doubtfully. It was the first time Baylee had had puppies, and they were having to learn as they went along, even though Lauren's mom had bought three different books on the subject.

"We need to leave for school," Dad

pointed out, checking his watch.

Lauren sighed. "I bet Baylee is going to have the puppies while I'm at school, and I really, really want to be here. Couldn't I just stay home? It's the last day of the semester; we're not going to actually do anything, are we?"

Mom shook her head. "No, you can't stay home. Besides, don't you want to say good-bye to all your friends? You won't see most of them for the next two months, remember."

Lauren frowned. It was true. She loved living way out in the country. Their home had been a farmhouse originally, and it had a huge yard. The old cowsheds had been made into her parents' office, and there was a barn across the yard that Lauren could play in. But there were bad things about it, too. She lived twenty minutes away from the town where her school was, and her best friend, Carolyn, lived in a town that was about twenty minutes beyond the school! So arranging to see Carolyn during vacations always meant a lot of planning.

Lauren grabbed her bag and the present she'd gotten for her teacher, Miss Ford, and took one last look at Baylee on the way out of the kitchen. The beautiful brown and white dog was squirming around on her cushion as though she couldn't quite get comfy.

"Can you just hold on until I get home?" Lauren pleaded. But Baylee looked up at her with big, mournful eyes. Lauren petted her lovingly.

"I see what you mean. You must really want to be back to your old self again. If it happens today, good luck, Baylee. It'll be worth it. You're going to have beautiful puppies soon."

"She's going to be very tired," Dad pointed out. "We'll have to take care of her. I remember doing all this with Rosie, my parents' dog, when I was just a little older than you. Now come on, Lauren, we're going to be late."

As they were bumping down the side street in the car toward the main road, Lauren asked, "How many puppies do you think Baylee will have?"

Dad shook his head. "Hard to tell—could be anything from one to 14, according to those books your mom bought. Rosie had only five."

Lauren frowned. "It can't just be one. Baylee is enormous."

"I think you're probably right—she is very big. I'd say we're looking at quite a few," Dad agreed.

He sighed as he noted her sparkling eyes and excited smile. "Lauren...."

"What?" Lauren looked over at him worriedly.

"Sweetheart, just remember that we aren't keeping these puppies. They're all going to new homes."

Lauren hesitated for a moment. "I know," she said quietly. She was silent for a little while and then added, "But we'll have them for a couple of months, won't we? That's all of summer vacation to play with them, and more."

Dad nodded. "Exactly. Of course

we'll miss them when they go, but it'll be easier if we remember that they aren't ours to keep."

"I won't forget," Lauren promised. "Oh, there's Carolyn, Dad! Can you let me out here? I can walk up the street to school with her and her mom, can't I?"

Dad pulled up, and Lauren jumped out of the car, waving to her best friend.

"Hi! How's Baylee? Has she had the puppies yet?" Carolyn asked breathlessly.

Lauren shook her head, then smiled. "Baylee was being really funny this morning. She kept messing around with her bed as if she were nesting. There might even be puppies when I get home!" she said, swinging her school bag excitedly.

"You're so lucky," said Carolyn. "Mom, can we have one of Baylee's puppies? Pleeeease?"

"Oh, Carolyn, you know I'd love one," said her mom, hitching Carolyn's baby sister, Amy, higher up on her hip. "But it just wouldn't be fair to have a dog. I'm busy with your sister, and your dad's at work during the day. A puppy would get lonely."

Carolyn sighed. "I suppose so."

"You'll be able to play with them when you come over during vacation," Lauren promised her. "And I won't get to keep the puppies, either. Dad was reminding me in the car."

Carolyn nodded. "Still, you'll have weeks and weeks to play with them all. Oh, there's the bell. See you later, Mom!"

The two girls ran into class and joined the crowd of children around Miss Ford, all begging her to open their good-bye present first.

Chapter Two
Puppies!

Lauren usually spent a long time chatting with all her friends at the end of school, but today she was desperate to see if the puppies had arrived. She dashed out onto the playground to find Dad waiting by the gate. Carolyn chased after her.

"Has Baylee had the puppies yet?" Lauren gasped. She'd been running so fast that she had to grab on to Dad's arm to stop herself from falling over.

Dad steadied her, laughing. "Yes."

"How many?" Lauren squeaked excitedly.

Dad smiled. "Guess."

Lauren frowned. "Five?"

"Nowhere near. 10!"

"Wow! 10 puppies?" Lauren turned around to Carolyn, her eyes round with amazement. "10? That's a *huge* litter!"

Carolyn laughed. "You'll have to think of 10 names!"

"That's going to be tricky," Dad said. Lauren gave him a worried look. He didn't sound quite as happy as she thought the owner of 10 puppies should. A sudden horrible thought hit her. Ten puppies was a lot—it must have been such hard work for Baylee, giving birth to so many. What if something was wrong with her? Lauren opened her mouth to ask, and then shut it again. She didn't want to talk about something so scary in the middle of the school playground.

Instead, she hugged Carolyn good-bye and promised to e-mail her a picture of the puppies later.

But as soon as she and Dad were heading for the car, she grabbed his hand. "Dad, is everything okay?"

"What do you mean?" Dad looked at her carefully.

"I just thought you seemed a little worried—after you told us there were so many puppies. Is Baylee all right?"

Dad gave her a hug. "Baylee's fine. I mean, she's exhausted, but she did really well. It's not Baylee...." He hesitated. "Lauren, one of the puppies is a lot smaller than the others. Mom and I—we're not sure this one will make it. It's such a tiny little thing, and when it was first born, we weren't even sure if it was breathing. Baylee had another puppy right after, and she didn't have time to lick the little puppy like she did with the others, or bite through its cord. I had to cut the cord myself, and I rubbed the puppy with a blanket to bring it around." He shook his head. "It did start to breathe, but it's not as strong as the other puppies, not by a long shot. It's just so tiny."

"Do you think it might die, Dad?" Lauren whispered.

Dad sighed. "I hope not—but we have to face the fact that it might."

"That's so sad." Lauren felt tears stinging her eyes. The poor little puppy.

"Nine healthy puppies is a great litter," Dad reminded her.

Lauren nodded. "I guess so. But I can't help worrying about the little one."

"I know. Me, too. Still, it might perk up. You never know."

Lauren crossed her fingers behind her back. She wanted Baylee to have all 10 of her wonderful puppies safe and well.

Lauren crept in the kitchen door. She was trying very hard not to upset Baylee.

But Baylee looked like she'd be impossible to disturb. She was stretched flat out on her side, fast asleep on the pile of old towels that Mom had put aside for her and the puppies to sleep on, in the special low wooden pen that Dad had made for them. They'd been worried that the puppies might fall off of Baylee's big cushion.

The puppies were all snuggled up next to their mom, fast asleep in a pile of heads and paws. Lauren knelt down beside the pen and tried to count them, but she couldn't figure out where one puppy ended and the next began.

She couldn't see which was the one that Dad was worried about, either.

"They're so tiny!" she whispered to Mom.

"I know, aren't they beautiful?" Mom beamed.

Lauren frowned. "They're all black-and-white! I can hardly see any brown on them at all. That's really weird, considering that Baylee is brown and white."

Mom shook her head. "I thought that, but then I looked it up in our beagle book, and it says they're usually born mostly black-and-white. The black might change to brown during the next few weeks, or stay as it is. Most beagles are black-and-white with brown patches—tricolor, it's called. Baylee's pretty rare, all brown and white."

"Look how pink their noses are," Lauren breathed. "And I can hear them snuffling! They're so adorable."

"Aren't they?" Dad agreed. "Oh, look, Baylee's waking up."

Lauren watched Baylee yawn and blink sleepily, and crouched closer to the pen, expecting Baylee to want to lick her hand. She was such a friendly dog, and she loved to cuddle up with Lauren—especially on the couch watching cartoons.

But today Baylee didn't seem to see her. She was only interested in her puppies. She nudged them awake, pushing them gently toward her tummy so they could start feeding.

"She was like that with me, too," Mom said. "Not interested. It's as if she only has eyes for her puppies now." She put her arm around Lauren's shoulders. "Don't worry. She'll only be like this for the first couple of weeks, until they open their eyes and start to move around. Then they won't need her so much, and she'll be our sweet Baylee again."

Lauren nodded. "Can I pick up one of the puppies?" she asked.

"We haven't touched them yet," Dad said. "We didn't want to upset Baylee."

Lauren peered at the pile of puppies as Baylee woke them up. "Which is the little one—the one that was having trouble breathing?" she asked anxiously. "Oh! I think I can see—is it the one Baylee's licking?"

Mom nodded. "Yes, that one's definitely a lot smaller than the others."

"Oh, look, you can see its little brown eyebrows!" Lauren said admiringly.

She edged closer to the pen, and Baylee glanced up, as if to check that she wasn't going to harm the puppies. Lauren shuffled back a little, and Baylee quickly went back to licking and nudging at the tiny puppy. The others were all feeding already—Lauren could hear the strange, wheezy squeak as they sucked. She giggled. "Look, Mom, that puppy is sitting on the other one's head!"

Mom smiled. "I don't think they mind as long as they're getting their mom's milk."

Dad was looking at one of the others. "Hey, puppy, I don't think that's going to do you much good," he chuckled. "Look, that big puppy is trying to suck Baylee's paw."

Baylee looked around at the sound of Dad's voice and spotted the confused puppy. She wrinkled her nose, and then gently pushed the puppy over to her tummy to feed with its brothers and sisters. Then she went back to trying to rouse the tiny puppy.

"That one really is a lot smaller than the others," Lauren said worriedly.

"And it's going to stay that way if it doesn't eat," Dad put in. "Oh, hang on, though. Look. Baylee got it moving."

The littlest puppy scrambled wearily, its paws waving. It was making sad squeaking sounds, as though it wished Baylee had left it to sleep, but at last it managed to burrow in among the rest of the litter.

"Is it feeding?" Mom asked hopefully.

"I think so." Lauren tried to listen for sucking sounds, but it was hard to tell with nine other puppies feeding at the same time. "Its head is moving back and forth, like the others."

Dad nodded. "That's good. I was getting worried."

Then Lauren winced as one of the other puppies kicked the tiny one in the stomach—not on purpose; the bigger puppy was just scrambling to get back to Baylee's milk. The tiny puppy lay there, kicking feebly, and then it seemed to go back to sleep. Lauren watched anxiously, willing it to wake up and feed again. But the littlest puppy just lay where it was, while its brothers and sisters wriggled and kicked for the best spot.

Chapter Three
Worrying

Hi Carolyn,

Here's a photo of the newborn puppies!
I bet you can't count all 10 in this pic-
ture, though, since they're all squeezed
in together. They're really beautiful, but
there's one tiny one that won't feed from
Baylee. I just hope it's going to get better.
Please come and see the puppies soon.
Love Lauren x

Lauren sent her e-mail to Carolyn and went downstairs to find Dad making dinner and Mom cuddling one of the puppies, while Baylee sat at the edge of the pen and kept a close eye on her.

"Oh, wow, she let you pick one up!"

Mom nodded. "But I was very careful. I washed my hands, and then I petted Baylee first, so that I didn't make the puppy smell like me. The book I was reading said that it was good to start handling puppies early, to get them used to people, but I don't want to worry Baylee. She doesn't seem too bothered, though—we thought she would be okay, since she's such a friendly dog." Mom ran her finger very gently down the snoozing puppy's back. "If you wash your hands, you can pet the puppy, too."

161

Lauren carefully washed her hands, and gave Baylee lots of attention first, petting her with both hands to get Baylee's scent on her fingers. Then she petted the puppy with one finger, like her mom had done. It felt like slightly damp velvet—and it was no bigger than one of the beanbag toy dogs she had on her windowsill upstairs. "It's so soft…," she breathed.

Baylee made a little snorting noise and lay down next to her puppies again, but she was still eyeing Lauren and her mom.

"Look how fat its tummy is," Mom pointed out. "This puppy is absolutely stuffed."

"I think we should put it back," Lauren said. "Baylee looks a little worried. But she hasn't growled or anything. She's such a good dog."

"And a good mother, too," Dad said from the stove. "She's taken to it so well."

Lauren's mom gently slipped the puppy back into the pen next to Baylee, who licked it all over. The puppy made a squeaking noise as Baylee's big tongue licked its head, but it didn't wake up.

"Where's the tiny one?" Lauren asked, trying to count the puppies.

Mom frowned. "I'm sure I saw it just a moment ago, and I think it had some more milk, which is really good. Apparently Baylee's milk is full of all sorts of good stuff on the day they're born. The puppies get all the benefit of the vaccinations she's had, that kind of thing."

"I can't see the little puppy now," Lauren muttered anxiously. "What if it's under all the others and they squash it?"

Mom knelt down next to her. "Isn't that it?" she asked, pointing to a puppy.

Lauren shook her head. "No, brown eyebrows, remember? That one's just black-and-white."

"Oh, yes." Mom edged around to the

other side of the pen. "It's here, behind Baylee. It must have gotten pushed out of the way by the others."

Lauren followed her, moving slowly so as not to disturb Baylee. "Is it okay?"

Baylee was watching carefully, and as soon as she realized what had happened, she wriggled around and tried to nudge the puppy over with her nose. But the puppy was fast asleep and didn't move. Baylee glanced up at Lauren and her mom, almost as though she wasn't quite sure what to do.

"Should we move the puppy for her?" Lauren asked, frowning.

Mom was starting to say, "Maybe we should…," when Baylee leaned down and picked up the tiny puppy in her mouth.

"Mom, what's Baylee doing?" Lauren whispered in horror.

"Don't worry," Mom soothed her. "It's fine. Dogs do that, Lauren; she won't hurt the puppy."

But it didn't look at all comfortable. The puppy's legs dangled out on either side of Baylee's mouth, and it wheezed and squeaked unhappily. Baylee swiftly tucked it next to her tummy and watched hopefully.

Lauren and Mom watched, too, and Dad left the pasta sauce he was stirring and came to peer over their shoulders, holding a wooden spoon covered in tomato sauce.

"It's feeding," Lauren whispered excitedly, seeing the little shoulders moving.

Mom nodded. "And since all the others are asleep, hopefully it'll be able to keep feeding for a while."

"Oh, that's good." Dad sighed with relief. "And good timing. Dinner is ready."

Lauren went to bed that night very reluctantly. She wanted to stay and watch the puppies, especially the tiniest one. She was still worried that it wasn't getting enough milk. Because it wasn't as big as the others, it couldn't wriggle its way back to Baylee when it got pushed away, like the others could. Instead of barging past its brothers and sisters, the littlest puppy would just whine miserably and go back to sleep.

"Can't I stay up a little longer? It's the first day of vacation tomorrow," Lauren begged.

"It's already an hour past bedtime!" Mom pointed out. "You can come down early in the morning to see them. But now you need to go to bed."

Lauren sighed, recognizing Mom's no-argument voice. Still, she was sure she wouldn't ever sleep.

Lauren woke up suddenly to find her bedroom in darkness. So she *had* fallen asleep after all.

She sat up, hugging her knees. What time was it? It felt like the middle of the night. She glanced at her luminous clock. Two o'clock in the morning. Lauren shuddered. No wonder it was so dark. She lay down again, but she didn't feel sleepy anymore. Something was worrying her, and she wasn't sure what it was. Then she realized—the puppies! Of course! How could she have forgotten about them?

She couldn't hear any noise from downstairs. Baylee and the puppies were probably fast asleep. But she couldn't stop worrying that something was wrong, and that was why she had woken up.

It wouldn't hurt to go and take a look, would it? Lauren smiled to herself—Mom had said she could come down early to see the puppies, after all. She probably hadn't meant quite this early, but still....

She got out of bed and crept over to her door, quickly pulling on her robe. As she ran across the landing to the stairs, she could hear her dad snoring. She hurried down the stairs and into the kitchen. She could hear little squeaks and sucking noises—the puppies were awake and feeding, but that wasn't really surprising. Lauren had been reading Mom's puppy books, and it said that for the first couple of weeks, they would need to feed every two hours.

Mom had left a small lamp from the living room plugged in on the counter so Baylee had some light for feeding the puppies. Baylee was lying on her side looking sleepy, but she thumped her tail gently on the floor of the pen when she saw Lauren.

"Hey, Baylee. I just came to see how you all are," Lauren whispered, kneeling beside the pen.

Baylee closed her eyes wearily as Lauren patted her head and leaned over to count the puppies. Then she counted them again. Only nine!

Where was the little puppy with the brown eyebrows?

"Oh, Baylee, where is it?" Lauren whispered, but Baylee was half-asleep, and she only twitched her tail.

Lauren checked behind Baylee, where the puppy had ended up before, but there was nothing there. She was sure the other puppies weren't lying on the little one, and it couldn't possibly have climbed out. Frantically, Lauren started to feel around the shadowy edges of the box.

"Oh!" Lauren gasped, as she touched something little and soft, pushed away in the corner. "There you are!" She picked up the puppy, waiting for it to squeak and complain, but it didn't make a sound. "Oh, no, I didn't wash my hands—I suppose it's too late now." Lauren lifted the puppy up to see better and realized that it was saggy and cold in her hands.

"Oh, no, please…," she muttered, and snuggled the puppy in a fold of her robe. "Mom! Dad!" she yelled, as she raced back up the stairs. "We need to call the vet!"

Chapter Four
Caring for Bitsy

"It woke up a little bit while I was holding it," Lauren explained to Mike, the vet. "Is it going to be all right?"

Mike put away his stethoscope and looked at the puppy thoughtfully. "You did really well to catch her when you did, Lauren. She's a she, by the way."

Lauren smiled, just a little. She had thought the puppy was a she—it was something about those cute brown eyebrows.

"It looks to me like she was slipping away," Mike went on, gently petting the puppy's head. "Puppies can't control how warm or cold they are; they need their mom to keep them warm. You cuddling her warmed her up again. The real problem is that she's not strong enough to feed properly by herself. But you could hand-rear her." He glanced up at Lauren, and her mom and dad. "I can't promise she'll make it. But it's worth a try. It's a lot of work, though."

Lauren's dad frowned. "What does hand-rearing mean, exactly? I've taken care of puppies before, but I've never had to hand-rear one. Would we feed her with a bottle?"

"A baby's bottle?" Lauren asked, looking at the tiny puppy. She was about the same size as a baby's bottle!

Mike shook his head. "No, a special puppy one. I've got one somewhere." He searched around in the drawer next to him. "Here it is, and here's some puppy milk replacement, and some information on hand-rearing." He handed Lauren's dad a jar of white powder and a pamphlet. "You mix it with water, just like baby formula. Puppies can't drink cows' milk; it has the wrong mix of nutrients for them."

Lauren's dad read the instructions on the jar. "Every two hours?" he asked, sounding slightly worried.

"Only for the first week," Mike reassured him. "After that you'll probably be able to leave her without a feeding through the middle of the night."

Dad rubbed his eyes wearily—it was now four o'clock in the morning. He and Mom ran their own mail-order business from home, and he'd been up late checking orders. He nodded. "Well, that's what we'll do." He glanced at Mom, who was looking anxious. "We can't not," he added gently.

Mom nodded. "Of course. It's going to be hard, though." She smiled at Lauren. "A little bit like when you were little."

Mike smiled. "But puppies grow faster than babies. They stop drinking their mom's milk at about seven weeks old. This little one should be feeding herself before you know it."

Lauren nodded. If it worked…. Mike hadn't sounded absolutely sure that it would. But Lauren had already saved this puppy once, and if she had anything to do with it, the little one was going to make it.

"I'll do it," she said to her parents. "The feeding, I mean. I don't mind."

"You can't get up every two hours in the middle of the night!" Mom said, sounding horrified.

"I can, Mom, please let me!" She looked toward Mike. "We should feed her now, shouldn't we? Do we have to use boiling water? Like Carolyn's mom uses for her little sister's bottles?"

Mike grinned at Lauren's parents. "It sounds like Lauren knows what she's doing."

Lauren beamed at him. She really wanted to help, but she had a feeling Mom and Dad weren't going to want her to do it. "Do we have to keep the puppy separate from the others?" she asked, trying hard to think of anything else they might need to know.

Mike frowned. "I would for tonight. She's obviously having trouble keeping warm, so she'll need a box and a hot-water bottle. The pamphlet shows you.

But after tonight, she'd be better off staying with her mom and the rest of the puppies, if she can. Just take her out for her feedings. Good luck! And if there are any problems, give us a call here at the animal hospital."

Mom went to prepare a box for the puppy, and Dad sat at the kitchen table reading the pamphlet that Mike had given them. "Small cardboard box. Blanket. Hot-water bottle," he muttered. "We should have thought

As soon as they got back home, Lauren ran to fill the kettle. The boiling water took forever to cool down, and Lauren kept wanting to blow on it.

Mom went to prepare a box for the puppy, and Dad sat at the kitchen table reading the pamphlet that Mike had given them. "Small cardboard box. Blanket. Hot-water bottle," he muttered. "We should have thought about all of this before, but it just never crossed my mind that we'd have so many puppies and Baylee wouldn't be able to feed them all. Ugh!"

"What?" Lauren turned around, still cradling the puppy.

Dad was making a face. "According to this, we're going to have to help the puppy poop, too. They don't do it themselves, apparently, and because Baylee won't be licking her after she's eaten, we'll have to wipe her bottom with wet cotton."

Lauren made a face back. That *was* a bit yucky. But it didn't turn her off. She was going to do everything necessary to keep the puppy going. Even if that meant making her poop.

"I think this water is cool enough to

mix the formula now. Not long until you can have some milk, Bitsy."

"Bitsy?" Mom asked. "When did you name her?"

Lauren looked up. "I didn't even notice I had! But don't you think she looks like a Bitsy?"

Mom nodded, but she was frowning, and Lauren bit her lip. She had a horrible feeling that Mom hadn't wanted her to name the tiny puppy in case she didn't make it.

Lauren carefully spooned the powder into the bottle and mixed in the water. "Wake up, little one…. Does it say how to hold her, Dad?"

Her dad skimmed through the instructions. "Flat, on her tummy, not on her back like a human baby. Here, look, on a towel." He laid a towel over Lauren's knees, and Lauren set Bitsy down on her tummy. Her paws splayed out and she scratched a little and let out a tiny squeak, unsure of what was going on.

"It's okay." Lauren picked up the bottle and gently put it against Bitsy's mouth.

"Squeeze the bottle a little," Mom suggested. "She doesn't know what it is. Let her taste a few drops of the milk."

All of a sudden, Bitsy started to suck eagerly as she tasted the milk in her mouth. Her tiny pink paws, with their little transparent claws, patted against Lauren's fingers, making her giggle. "Wow, she was ready for that."

Bitsy took only five minutes to down the bottle.

"Goodness, should we give her some more?" Mom asked.

Lauren shook her head. "No, this is how much Mike said for now. The powder container tells how much to give during an entire day based on the size of the puppy, and then you have to divide that up between the feedings." She gave a big yawn, and on her knee, Bitsy did the same.

Mom laughed. "I think we should all go to bed. Especially if we have to be up at six-thirty to feed her again."

Lauren looked up at her mom hopefully. "Mom, my bedroom is nice and warm, and if I have her box in there, I can keep an eye on her...."

"But we have to feed her so early. You don't want to get up at six-thirty during vacation!" Dad smiled.

"I do, I really do!" Lauren promised. "I was the one who woke up and found her, Dad. I really want to help."

Dad looked over at Lauren's mom. "What do you think, Annie?"

Mom sighed. "I suppose so. But only for tonight, Lauren. Tomorrow, when she's a little stronger, Bitsy can go back with Baylee and the other puppies."

Lauren nodded eagerly and picked up the cardboard box. Inside, Bitsy was snuggling up against the well-wrapped hot-water bottle. Lauren thought she looked happier than she had all day. She padded back up the stairs, yawning uncontrollably. She set the box down next to her bed and fell asleep listening to the tiny wheezy breaths from inside the box.

It was really hard to get up when Dad came in at six-thirty, but Lauren dragged herself out of bed and carried Bitsy's box downstairs to watch Dad prepare her next bottle. The trip downstairs hadn't disturbed Bitsy at all, she noticed with a smile. The puppy was still snoozing peacefully next to the cooling hot-water bottle.

In the kitchen, Baylee was out of the puppy pen looking hungry, and Lauren fed her while Dad boiled water in the kettle.

"Can I feed Bitsy again?" Lauren begged, and Dad handed her the bottle.

"You might as well—you certainly seemed to have the knack earlier!"

Going downstairs might not have woken Bitsy, but the smell of the puppy formula certainly did, and she was gasping and squeaking with excitement as soon as Lauren held the bottle to her mouth.

After she'd cleaned Bitsy up, Lauren took her over to Baylee. She and Dad hovered anxiously, not too close to the puppy pen, watching to see how Baylee would react.

"I hope Bitsy will be all right," Lauren muttered. "It said in that pamphlet that sometimes the mom tries to lick the human smell away and accidentally hurts the puppy."

Dad put an arm around her shoulders. "We'll watch really carefully," he promised. "And it's not as if Baylee's a dog who lives outside and doesn't really know people that well. She's part of our family. Hopefully our smell won't upset her too much."

"Look!" Lauren whispered.

Baylee was sniffing thoughtfully at Bitsy, and Lauren held her breath as Baylee started to lick the little puppy. But Baylee didn't look at all upset, just a little surprised.

Lauren giggled. "I think Baylee's so worn out that she hardly noticed Bitsy was gone!"

Over the next few days, Lauren was sure that Bitsy had started to recognize her. If Bitsy started squeaking in her box, she would calm down as soon as Lauren picked her up, but not if it was Mom or Dad. Lauren knew it was probably just that Bitsy recognized her by smell as the person who usually fed her, but it still made her feel special. She couldn't wait for Bitsy to open her eyes so that the puppy could see her as well as smell her.

Mom and Dad were supposed to be taking turns doing the night feedings, but Lauren couldn't help waking up when she heard the alarm go off in their bedroom. And once she was awake, she just couldn't stay in bed. Mom even stopped saying anything about it by the end of their second night of puppy-rearing.

Bitsy was putting on weight now,

although not as fast as the other
puppies, who were round and glossy-
furred. She adored her feedings, but
Lauren suspected she might always be a
little smaller than her brothers and sisters.

Bitsy squeaked and sucked at Lauren's
fingers as Lauren scooped her up. She
knew Lauren's scent, and she was sure
it was time for Lauren to feed her, and
she was so, so hungry.

Lauren giggled as Bitsy's little pink paws flailed around. "I'm just waiting for it to cool down. You don't want to burn your mouth!"

Bitsy squeaked even louder. Where was the milk?

"Okay, okay, here you go."

Bitsy sighed happily and settled down to sucking. That was much better.

After the first week, Lauren and her parents could leave Bitsy for six hours in the middle of the night without a feeding. Dad said he'd do the midnight feeding on his own—he was used to staying up late working anyway. Lauren had to admit that it was really nice to get a good night's sleep again, even though she still had to get up super-early for Bitsy's morning feeding.

Carolyn came to visit the puppies when they were about two weeks old.

"Can I feed Bitsy?" she asked hopefully. "That photo you sent me of you feeding her was so cute. She's even more beautiful now that her eyes are open, though."

"She is, isn't she?" Lauren agreed, handing Carolyn the bottle.

Bitsy watched Lauren the whole time she was feeding, and Lauren could tell she was confused why somebody else was holding her bottle.

"You have to burp her now, like your mom burps Amy," Lauren told Carolyn when Bitsy had finished.

Now that the puppies were two weeks old, their eyes were open, although they still hadn't really started to move around much. The really exciting thing was that their markings were starting to come through. Bitsy had more brown on her face now, not just her pretty eyebrows, and all the puppies were changing every day.

Even though the puppies were still too tiny to really play with, Carolyn didn't want to leave when her mom came to pick her up.

Lauren waved good-bye from the door and sighed as Carolyn's car disappeared down the street. She really missed seeing her best friend every day.

"Lauren, I've got some really exciting news," her mom began as she came back into the kitchen. "Hey, what's the matter?"

"I just wish I could see Carolyn more often during vacations, that's all. E-mails and phone calls aren't the same as having a friend close by."

Her mom gave her a hug. "This is going to be extra-good news for you, then." She beamed at Lauren. "We've rented out the cottage. To a family with a boy the same age as you!"

Lauren blinked. The cottage was

on the other side of the orchard, just beyond the barnyard. The old tenant had left a long time ago, and Lauren had forgotten they were trying to find someone new.

"His name is Sam Martin, and he has a little sister named Susan. Isn't that wonderful? You'll have a friend really close by!"

Lauren nodded slowly, but she wasn't sure it was all that wonderful. What if she didn't like this boy? And even if she did, he wouldn't be as good a friend as Carolyn.

Chapter Five
A New Friend

"Oh, that sounds like the Martins at the door!" Mom bustled around the kitchen, putting the kettle of water on the stove. "Would you open it, Lauren?"

It was two weeks after Mom had shared the news about the new neighbors moving in, and they'd said they were going to stop by that afternoon. Lauren still couldn't help wishing it was a girl her age rather than a boy. And she didn't want some strange boy and his little sister messing around with Bitsy and upsetting her. Instead of opening the door, she quickly dashed upstairs with Bitsy and stashed her in the box she'd slept in on the first night. Mom still let her take Bitsy upstairs occasionally, and Bitsy couldn't get out of the box yet, although she really liked trying.

Bitsy whined in surprise as Lauren put her down. What was happening? She had been enjoying a nice cuddle, and now she was being left all on her own! She stood up with her paws against the edge of the box, scratching hard. Where was Lauren? She whimpered miserably.

Lauren ran back downstairs and tried

to look friendly as Mom introduced her to Mrs. Martin and Sam, a blond-haired boy who looked just as embarrassed as she felt. Sam's dad was still sorting things out at the house, and his little sister was asleep, Mrs. Martin said.

Sam cuddled one of the puppies, the big boy that they had named Buster, and didn't really say much. Lauren was just hoping that they might go soon—surely they must have a lot of unpacking to do. But then her mom nudged her and said meaningfully, "Why don't you show Sam around the farm?"

Lauren frowned. It was almost time to feed Bitsy, and she didn't want to, anyway!

Her mom glared at her, and she gave a

tiny sigh and turned to Sam. "Come on. You can bring Buster, if you like."

Sam nodded and followed her out into the yard. "He's really nice. Is he your favorite?"

Lauren shook her head.

"Don't you have a favorite? He'd be mine. He's great." Sam snuggled Buster up under his chin.

Lauren didn't know what to say.

It would sound silly to admit that she'd hidden Bitsy. "I like them all," she said, a bit vaguely.

Lauren trailed around the farm, showing Sam the orchard, and the old barn on the other side of the yard. There were a few bales of hay in it still, and she liked to hide in there sometimes.

"This is cool. I bet the puppies would love it in here," said Sam.

Lauren nodded. "They haven't been outside much yet, but Dad is making a wire run so they can play in the orchard."

Sam looked up. "Oh, that's my mom calling. I guess we have to go and unpack."

He handed Buster to Lauren, and they headed back to the farmhouse. Lauren supposed Sam was okay, really—at least he liked the puppies—but she didn't think they were going to be best friends or anything, which was obviously what Mom was hoping.

"He was nice, wasn't he?" Mom asked as they waved good-bye to Sam and his mom. "Gosh, look at Buster!" She tickled the puppy under the chin. "He's huge. I need to put an ad in the local paper about new homes for the puppies. And there are a couple of good puppy websites, too."

Lauren swallowed. Her heart seemed to have suddenly jumped into her throat. New homes! She had almost forgotten about that—she had wanted to forget.

"But they're only a month old, Mom!" she cried.

"I know. But puppies go to their new owners at about eight weeks, and people don't just show up and take a puppy home. We'll have to let them come and see the puppies—and we need to meet them to make sure we like them." She hugged Lauren. "We're not going to give Baylee's beautiful puppies to just anyone, sweetheart, don't worry."

Lauren nodded. "But—but not Bitsy?" she asked quickly. "She isn't big enough yet, Mom."

Mom nodded thoughtfully. "You're probably right. Bitsy will have to be a little older than the others when she goes. Not much, though, I don't think. You've done so well feeding her; she's catching up to them." She looked at Lauren. "I know you really love Bitsy, and it'll be hard for you to say good-bye, but you'll still have Baylee, remember."

Lauren buried her nose in Buster's soft fur. She loved Baylee, of course she did. But Bitsy would have died if Lauren hadn't woken up that first night. It felt like she and Bitsy belonged together. But Lauren just didn't think she could explain that to Mom.

She put Buster back in the puppy pen and ran upstairs to get Bitsy. When she opened her bedroom door, Bitsy scratched at the side of the box with her claws, squeaking frantically.

"Oh, I'm sorry. I went off and left you, didn't I?" Lauren scooped up the puppy, her eyes filling with tears. "I didn't mean to." She sighed, feeling Bitsy wriggle and squirm against her neck. "I don't ever want to leave you. But I'm not going to, am I? You're going to leave me. Oh, Bitsy, I don't want you to go!"

205

Summer vacation went by so quickly! Lauren thought. She could hardly believe that there was less than a week to go until school started! She supposed it was because she'd been busy all the time taking care of Bitsy and Baylee, and the other puppies.

Bitsy's brothers and sisters loved the little outdoor run that Lauren's dad had made for them, and they spent a lot of time out there now. Lauren's mom had put a photo of them all bouncing around on the grass on the pet website where she was advertising them to new owners.

Lauren wasn't sure about letting Bitsy go out in the run yet—she was still so much smaller than the other puppies, and Lauren was worried that they might hurt her with their rough and tumble games.

"Mom, can I take Bitsy out to play in the orchard, if I'm really careful not to let her run off?"

Her mom put down the phone. "Yes, that's fine. Although I'm sure she'd be all right in the run with the others, you know. She's a lot bigger now."

Lauren sighed. She supposed Bitsy was catching up. But she still wouldn't feed from Baylee like they did. Dad said she liked her special bottles too much. They wouldn't have to do the bottle feedings for too much longer, though. Now that the puppies were five weeks old, they were all eating solid food, too. Lauren loved to watch them eat.

The first few meals had gone everywhere but into the puppies' mouths, and Baylee had ended up having most of it as she'd licked it off the puppies. They had the same dry food as Baylee, but mixed with the puppy milk Bitsy had, and they always ended up with mush caked all over their ears.

"Who was on the phone?" Lauren asked as she finished her toast. "It wasn't someone about the puppies, was it?"

"No, it was just Nicky, Sam's mom. We'd talked about sharing the rides to and from school next week, and she wanted to know if we'd rather do morning or afternoon. I said we'd pick you up in the afternoon. Is that okay?

I like hearing about your day."

Lauren gaped at her. "Sam's going to my school?" she asked.

"Well, of course he is. Yours is the only school close by."

"He's not in my class, is he?"

"No, he's in the other class." Her mom frowned. "His mom and I talked about it when they came over. Didn't you hear us?"

Lauren shook her head. She supposed she'd been too busy being grumpy about having to entertain Sam. And now she had to share rides to school with him! She knew it would make less work for Mom and Dad, but she didn't want to share her car rides; she liked having the time to talk to them.

Angrily, she picked up Bitsy and a ball

from the puppy pen and stomped out into the yard.

Bitsy squirmed excitedly in Lauren's arms, sniffing all the interesting new smells. She'd been everywhere in the house with Lauren, but this was different. A butterfly fluttered past, and she yapped at it in delight. When they got to the orchard, which had a brick wall all around it, Lauren gently put her down on the grass.

Bitsy looked up at her, not sure what she was supposed to do. She gave an inquiring little whine.

"Go play!" Lauren rolled the ball, and Bitsy chased after it, yapping. She tried to sink her teeth into it, but it was just too big, and she ended up rolling over on top of the ball with a squeak of dismay.

Bitsy bounced up and went off sniffing around in the grass until she came to a plant with huge leaves. She licked a leaf thoughtfully, and then seized it in her teeth, pulling hard. It sprang back, and she jumped around yapping fiercely, until Lauren nearly choked with laughter.

All of a sudden there was a heavy thud, and a soccer ball bounced over the orchard wall and thumped onto the grass right next to Bitsy, who whimpered in fright. She scampered over to Lauren.

Lauren snatched Bitsy up in one arm, grabbed the ball with the other, and ran across to the wall to find Sam peering over it.

"Hey! You almost hit Bitsy with that! What are you doing?" Lauren snapped.

"Sorry! I was just kicking the ball around…." Sam looked guilty.

"You could have hurt her!" Lauren told him as she shoved the ball into his hands.

"Sorry…," Sam muttered again, and he walked away with his shoulders hunched over.

Lauren almost felt sorry for yelling at him, but then Bitsy wriggled into her neck, whimpering, and Lauren felt angry all over again.

When school started the next week, Lauren had to share rides with Sam, as her mom had arranged, but Lauren hardly talked to him. She didn't really know what to say, and Sam seemed shy of her. She supposed it was because of the way she'd talked to him in the orchard.

It was great being back at school and seeing all her friends again, but she really missed Bitsy and the other puppies.

"Are they big enough for new homes yet?" Carolyn asked at recess.

"Mom has people coming to see them already, and they can leave Baylee after next week, she says. People have already chosen six of them. Not Bitsy, though; she's still too little." *Thank goodness*, she added silently. Over the weekend, a family had come to see the puppies, and the little girl had picked up Bitsy, saying she wanted her. Lauren had felt sick watching. Luckily, Mom had seen her horrified face and explained that

Bitsy was too little to go for a few more weeks. The family had chosen two girl puppies named Daisy and Dani instead. But afterward, Mom had sat down with Lauren and hugged her, and explained that she was going to have to let Bitsy go sometime.

"You'll really miss her, won't you?" Carolyn said, putting her arm through Lauren's, and Lauren nodded.

"Couldn't you ask your mom and dad if you can keep her?" Carolyn suggested.

"I wish I could," Lauren whispered. "They've always said we can't, that we already have Baylee. But I just can't bear to think of Bitsy belonging to someone else."

Chapter Six
Where's Bitsy?

Bitsy watched the strange boy cuddling Buster and wondered who he was. There were a lot of other people in her kitchen, too, but they all seemed friendly. Everyone who had come to the house over the last two weeks had wanted to pet her and her brothers and sisters, and play with them. It was fun, but it was confusing, too. She had a feeling that this boy was going to take Buster away. He had been here before, and this time he had picked Buster up right away, and Buster had wagged his tail and yipped happily, the way Bitsy did when Lauren cuddled her.

If Buster went away with this boy, then she would be the only puppy left. Daisy and Dani had gone with a little girl the day before. The girl's mother had put them in a special box with a wire front, and Lauren had taken her out to see Daisy and Dani drive off in a car. Lauren had hugged her extra tight, and seemed really sad, although she'd cheered up and giggled when Bitsy licked her ear.

Bitsy missed rolling over and over with all the others, now that it was just

Buster and her. She still had Lauren to play with, of course, and that was her favorite thing. But was she going to go somewhere, too, like all her brothers and sisters? She didn't want to. She wanted to stay here with Lauren.

The boy snuggled Buster under his chin and then turned to put him into a carrier like the one Daisy and Dani went away in. Bitsy watched them go out into the yard, and then she looked around the puppy run, with its rumpled blankets and scattered toys, and howled a big beagle howl.

"Oh! Did Buster go today?" Lauren asked in surprise when she got home from playing at Carolyn's house.

"Yes, there's only Bitsy left," her mom answered. "Did you have a good time?"

"Yes, it was great," Lauren replied, only half listening. She was looking at Bitsy curled up asleep on the fluffy bed at one side of the puppy run. She seemed so tiny and alone.

Bitsy woke up and stared around her at the empty run, looking confused. She let out a tiny whimper and staggered to her feet, sniffing around the pen. Baylee leaned over and licked her gently, and Bitsy stopped whimpering, but she still looked uncertain.

Mom put her arm around Lauren. "She's gotten so much bigger, hasn't she? And you can really see all the brown coming out on her now. She's going to be so beautiful. You did really well with the hand-rearing, Lauren; it was such hard work. Dad and I are very proud of you, you know."

"Thanks," Lauren muttered. She was proud of what she had done with Bitsy, too, but she had a horrible feeling that she knew what was coming next.

"I know you'll miss her, sweetheart, but she's ready to go to a new home," Mom said gently. "She's hardly bothering with her bottles, and she's eating dry food now."

Lauren nodded and sniffed. It was

all true, but that didn't make it any easier. She pulled away from her mom with a muttered "Sorry!," picked up Bitsy, who squeaked in surprise, and fled upstairs.

Lauren was really looking forward to Friday and the start of the weekend. She enjoyed being back at school, but she missed Bitsy so much—and she wasn't sure how much more time they had together.

Her dad had picked up Sam and her as usual, and they sat in the back seat while Dad tried to ask cheerful questions about how Sam was settling in, and Sam kept saying things like,

"Okay," and "Fine, thanks."

They dropped Sam off, and then Lauren ran inside to say hello to Bitsy.

The phone was ringing as she went into the kitchen, and her mom yelled from upstairs, "Can you answer that, Lauren? I'm just making the beds!"

Lauren grabbed the phone, hoping it wasn't an order for her parents' camping supplies company, as she always worried she'd get them wrong.

"Hello?"

"Is this Mrs. Woods? With the beagle puppies?"

"Oh! Yes—I mean, I'm her daughter," Lauren explained.

"Oh, good. Do you have any puppies left? I just saw the website."

Lauren swallowed. This lady might

end up being Bitsy's owner. All of a sudden, her eyes filled with tears. "There is one puppy left," she said, making her voice sound very doubtful.

"Is there something wrong with it?" The lady on the phone sounded worried.

"Well…. She was the smallest of the litter, much smaller than the others. We had to hand-rear her."

"Oh, dear. Well, if she's not healthy, I think I'll try someone else. Thanks anyway."

Lauren pressed the button to end the call with a shaky hand and put down the phone.

But she couldn't answer the phone every time someone called….

Still feeling really guilty, Lauren took Bitsy out into the yard to play. She threw a ball for Bitsy to chase, and she raced up and down the yard with excited squeaks.

"Lauren!" Mom was calling from the small, grassy area next to the house where the clothesline was. "Can you help me hang the clothes, please?"

Lauren sighed. Hanging the clothes was one of the jobs she did to earn her allowance. "Sorry, Bitsy," she said, picking her up. "You go in the run, okay? I'll be back soon."

Bitsy stared after her, whining. Lauren had left the ball on the grass, and there were no toys in the run. Bitsy ran up and down, sniffing at the wire, then scratched at it, wondering if she could get out and fetch the ball. She stuck a small paw through the wire fence, but the ball was too far away to reach.

Yapping angrily, Bitsy scratched at the wire again, standing up on her hind paws. Her claws caught in the wire. She looked at them thoughtfully, and unhooked them. Then she stretched up higher, clinging on tight. She was climbing! Wriggling and scrambling, she worked her way up the side of the run. She teetered on the top, not quite sure what to do next. All at once, she let go and scrambled down the other side, landing in a little heap.

She sprang up and shook herself excitedly. There it was—her ball! She chased after it, pushing it along with her front paws, and followed the ball as it rolled through the front gate and out into the yard.

Ten minutes later, Lauren dashed back, eager to keep playing with Bitsy, only to find that Bitsy wasn't there.

She stood staring at the run. The fence was about two feet high—surely Bitsy was too small to climb out!

"Bitsy! Bitsy!" Lauren cried, as she ran all around the run.

But the little puppy was nowhere to be found.

Chapter Seven
A Plan

Bitsy padded across the yard and set off exploring around the other side of the orchard wall. She'd abandoned the ball in favor of all the other interesting things she could smell. Maybe she'd find Lauren if she went down here, too. She spotted a snail climbing up the wall and watched it round-eyed. She went closer and sniffed. It had an odd smell, and she decided it wasn't for eating.

"Hey! Bitsy!" Bitsy jumped, and looked up. That wasn't Lauren's voice.

It was the boy, Sam, holding a big ball. She'd seen him before when he came to the house to pick up Lauren in the mornings. She sniffed his fingers in a friendly sort of way. Maybe he would play with her....

"Are you supposed to be out here on your own?" he asked. "I bet you're not."

"Bitsy! Bitsy!" There was a distant voice calling, sounding worried.

"You're definitely not," Sam told Bitsy. "That sounds like Lauren looking for you."

Bitsy could hear Lauren, too, but she wasn't quite sure where she was. She whimpered anxiously.

"It's all right. Let's find Lauren, okay?" Sam looked down at her, and Bitsy pawed his foot eagerly.

"Come on. Good girl." Sam put the ball down and picked up Bitsy. He walked quickly toward the yard. "Hey, Lauren, I've got her!"

Lauren came dashing out of the front gate. She grabbed Bitsy, hugging her tightly while Bitsy whined with delight. "Oh, you're terrific, Sam! I was really worried. She must have climbed out of her run. Thanks!"

"Beagles are really good at escaping." Sam nodded, and Lauren looked at him in surprise. "I really like dogs," he explained. "We can't have one, because Dad is allergic, but I've got a ton of dog books. And I once saw a video on a website of a beagle climbing out of a huge pen."

"Oh." Lauren suddenly felt really ashamed. She'd been going to school with Sam every day, and she hadn't asked him anything about himself, or said a single friendly thing. "It's wonderful that you found her. What if she'd gone out into the road?"

Sam nodded. "I can't imagine losing a dog like that," he agreed. "It would be awful."

Lauren's eyes suddenly welled up.

"I'm sorry! I didn't mean to make you cry!" Sam said, looking horrified.

"It's okay," Lauren gulped. "It's just— you don't understand…." She wiped her hand across her eyes, while Bitsy licked at her cheek anxiously.

"Bitsy isn't mine. Not forever. She's going to have a new home, just like the other puppies. And I can't stand the thought of not having her anymore."

"Oh, wow," Sam muttered. "I thought you were keeping her, when she stayed and all the others went. And she's with you all the time."

"I've always known she'd have to go, like her brothers and sisters," Lauren whispered. "I still have Baylee, and of course I love her, but I've spent so much time with Bitsy, because we hand-reared her. It's going to be awful when she leaves. It was bad enough when people came for the others, but Bitsy is special." She opened the orchard gate and gently shooed Bitsy in. "Want to come and play with her?" she said.

Sam nodded and followed her. "Has anyone come to see Bitsy?" he asked.

Lauren shook her head. "Someone called earlier, and I sort of mentioned how Bitsy was the smallest one of the litter and made this lady think she wasn't very healthy...."

She glanced at Sam, not sure what he'd think, but Sam looked impressed.

"I felt really guilty afterward," Lauren admitted. "And I can't keep turning people away."

Sam looked thoughtful. "There must be something you can do. I'll help you." He looked at Bitsy, who was destroying an apple that had fallen on the ground. "You can't lose her," he said firmly.

Lauren smiled. He sounded so certain that it made her feel a little bit better.

The next morning, Sam knocked on the kitchen door while Lauren was finishing her breakfast, and slipping cornflakes to Baylee and Bitsy, who were sitting on either side of her chair.

"Good morning, Mrs. Woods," he said politely to Lauren's mom. "I was just wondering if Lauren wanted to come out and play."

"I'm sure she does!" Lauren's mom said, looking delighted, and Lauren rolled her eyes at Sam, who tried not to laugh.

"I'm popular, then," he said quietly as they went across the yard with Bitsy and Baylee on their leashes.

"Mom thinks it's really nice for me

to have a friend living close by." Lauren swallowed nervously. "I'm sorry I haven't been very friendly. I was a little angry when Mom arranged the rides and everything—like I didn't have a choice."

"Me, too!" Sam agreed. "My mom kept going on about how lucky I was, and I was like, she's a girl and I've never even met her! I'm sorry," he added. "Anyway, I've got a plan!"

"You do?" Lauren asked eagerly. "Tell me."

Sam sat down on the rusty old tractor that had been abandoned on the edge of the field and beamed. "I think we should adopt Bitsy ourselves! I have $30 of birthday money left for dog food, shots, and things like that, if I could share Bitsy. Take her for walks sometimes and stuff. It's the closest I'll get to having a dog, after all."

Lauren nodded slowly. "I have the money my grandma gave me at the beginning of summer vacation, but I've been so busy with the puppies I never got around to spending it. That's $50 so far. Puppies don't need more than $100 worth of stuff, do they? But how are we going to get the rest of the money?"

Sam grinned. "I thought we could pick the apples from the orchard and sell them. We could set up a stand on that big patch of grass where the road down to the farm ends. It's close enough to the main road for people to see us and stop."

Lauren jumped off the tractor wheel. "That's a great plan! Mom and Dad never have time to pick them, so they won't mind. I'll go get some buckets."

It took a while to pick the apples, because a lot of them had holes from wasps getting to them, and those had to be thrown on the compost heap— but eventually they had three buckets of really nice-looking apples. When they went back home for lunch, Lauren grabbed a handful of freezer bags from the kitchen. Sam found an old folding table in the big shed at the back of the cottage, and he borrowed one of the boxes from the move to make into cardboard signs.

Then Lauren had another idea. "You start selling the apples. I just remembered something—Mom's always saying I should go through my old soft toys. We can sell those, too. Here, you take Bitsy.

I'm going to head back home and get them."

By the time she struggled down the road with a garbage bag full of stuffed bears and dogs, Sam was looking very pleased with himself. "I've already sold three bags!" He'd made the signs as well, and tied a couple onto the bushes on both sides of the road.

"That's great! Can you please help me put the toys on the grass in front of the table? They'll make people stop and take a look."

"Bitsy and Baylee have been making people stop, too. They've had a lot of attention."

It turned out that the toys were almost more popular than the apples. Lauren even had to go back and find some more soft toys that she hadn't been planning to get rid of, but she didn't mind giving up her toy beanbag dogs if it meant she could keep her real one.

"How much money have we made?" Sam asked as they packed up at dinnertime.

"Twenty dollars!" Lauren beamed. "So that's $70 altogether. And there are a lot more apples we can pick. But I don't think I have any more old toys."

Lauren's mom and dad were so happy that she was playing with Sam that they didn't ask what they'd been doing all afternoon. And they didn't mind at all when she and Sam and the dogs disappeared again the next morning.

It was the middle of the morning, and they were doing very well, when a car pulled up by the stand.

"Would you like some apples?" Sam asked, sounding very professional, and the man smiled and dug around in his pockets for some change.

"Actually, I'm looking for Redhills Farm," he explained as Lauren handed the apples through the car window.

"It's down there," Lauren pointed.

"Thanks. I came to look at a beagle puppy—is that the mom? She's beautiful." He nodded at Baylee, who was sitting by Lauren's side. He couldn't see Bitsy, as she was curled up asleep, half inside Sam's hoodie top.

"Y-yes…," Lauren stammered, and the man waved and drove away.

Sam and Lauren stared at each other in horror. The man had come for Bitsy! They were too late!

Chapter Eight
The Best News

"What are we going to do?" Lauren whispered. "We can't let him have her. We really can't! Mom didn't say anyone was coming. He must have just showed up."

Sam nodded. "We almost have enough money, too. It's not fair."

Lauren looked at him, frowning. "If Bitsy's not there, he can't see if he likes her…," she suggested slowly.

"You mean we should just stay here?" Sam asked.

Lauren shook her head. "No. Because he's seen us, and Mom knows we have Bitsy. We have to hide. Come on!"

"Where are we going?" Sam asked.

"I don't know yet. Let's just get away from here."

"Okay." Sam zipped up his hoodie and used it like a bag to carry Bitsy, while Lauren grabbed Baylee's leash.

Bitsy woke up as they ran back down the road, as Sam was jiggling her around inside his top. She gave an indignant squeak and tried to wriggle out.

Lauren turned back. "I'll take her. She'll be quieter with me. Shhh, Bitsy!" Bitsy snuggled gratefully into Lauren's arms as Sam handed her over.

As they peered around the corner of the barn, they saw the man's car parked in the yard. The top half of the back door was open, and they could see him talking to Lauren's mom in the kitchen.

"Let's hide in the barn," Lauren said quickly. "If we go behind the bales of straw, we'll still be able to see if they come out."

They sneaked through the open doors and settled themselves at the back of the barn.

"Shhh! I can hear my mom," Lauren whispered.

"Lauren! Lauren!" They could just see Lauren's mom, looking a little embarrassed. "She's probably in the orchard, playing with Bitsy," she said.

"I'm sorry. I should've called first," the man said. "I saw the ad and thought I'd just stop by, since I was coming this way. There were two children up at the top of the road with a beagle."

"Oh! Well, that would be Lauren and Sam. I hope they haven't gone along the road. Lauren knows not to. I'd better go up there and find them. You stay here and drink your tea."

Lauren sank back behind the straw bales. "She's going to be upset when she sees we aren't there," she said slowly.

"Do you want to let your mom know where we are?" Sam asked.

Lauren chewed her lip uncertainly, but then Bitsy woke up again inside Sam's hoodie and wriggled out. She gave a little yap and looked up at Lauren with her big brown eyes. She looked so beautiful that Lauren knew she couldn't bear to let her go. "No," she said firmly. "He'll give up waiting soon, hopefully."

Bitsy climbed off Lauren's lap and went sniffing around the floor, and nudging up against Baylee, who was quietly curled up on a pile of straw. Baylee yawned and licked Bitsy half-heartedly. It looked like she just wanted to sleep.

Bitsy could smell delicious smells all

around the barn. She padded off around the edge of the bale to investigate, and Lauren and Sam both dived to grab her, which made Baylee bark.

"Shhh!" Lauren hissed, putting her finger to her lips, and Baylee gave her a confused look. "I'm sorry, Baylee, sweetie. But we have to be quiet, okay?"

Sam put Bitsy in his lap and started to wave a piece of straw for her to chase. "I don't think we can keep this little one quiet, though," he said as Bitsy squeaked delightedly and growled at the straw.

"They might not hear from out there. Oh, there's Mom. She looks worried," Lauren said guiltily.

Lauren's mom went into the house and obviously told the man she couldn't find Lauren and Bitsy, because he came out and got into his car.

"I'm so sorry," Lauren's mom said.

Lauren thought the man looked disappointed, but she was more worried about the anxious look on her mom's face.

The man handed Lauren's mom a piece of paper. "Here's my phone number, anyway. If you could give me a call." Then he drove off down the road.

Bitsy growled at the straw again. Sam had stopped waving it around, and she was getting bored. She whined loudly and tugged the hem of Lauren's jeans with her teeth. She wanted them to play properly.

"Should we come out, now that he's gone?" Sam asked.

Lauren wanted to, especially since she could hear her mom calling for her dad, who was working in the office at the back of the house. Now they'd both be searching for her. But she shook her head. "What if they just call the man to come back?" She nibbled her nails. "I think we have to wait a little longer."

They could hear Lauren's mom and dad going around the house shouting her name. Finally, Baylee started whining. "I know, Baylee," Lauren whispered. "I'm hungry, too."

"I'm starving," Sam muttered, and then he gasped as he heard a different voice. "That's my mom!"

Sam's mom came running into the yard carrying Susan. Susan was crying and calling, "Sam?"

Sam and Lauren exchanged a guilty glance.

"I'm sorry, but I have to go. Susan looks really upset…." Sam was getting to his feet. "You stay, and I'll say I wasn't with you."

"It's okay. I'm coming, too," Lauren told him. "And I promise you won't get into trouble. I'll say it was all my idea." They crept over to the barn door and peered out anxiously. Baylee looked around their legs, unsure what was going on. Only Bitsy was happy and squeaked excitedly to see everyone.

"Sam!"

"Lauren!"

"Didn't you hear us calling you? We've been shouting for a while!" Lauren's mom hugged her. "We had no idea where you were!"

Susan struggled down from her mom's arms and ran to hug Sam.

"Were you in the barn the whole time?" Dad asked, looking from Lauren to Sam and back again.

"Um, yes…," Lauren admitted.

"So you were hiding on purpose," Dad said.

Lauren glanced worriedly at Sam, and then said, very fast, "That man had come to adopt Bitsy, and I didn't want him to."

Mom blinked. "He was very nice. He already has one beagle and wanted another. He was really disappointed when we couldn't find you."

"Sam, I can't believe you frightened us all like that," his mom said angrily.

"I think we'd all better go inside," Dad said firmly. "I want to understand what's going on here." He shooed Sam and Lauren and the two dogs into the kitchen, where Baylee and Bitsy went eagerly to their food bowls. "Sit down, you two. Now, explain. What was wrong with that man that made you decide to do something so silly? He seemed like he'd be a really good owner."

"Nothing…," Lauren began haltingly.

"It wasn't him," Sam put in. "We didn't want anyone to have Bitsy. Look." He dug in his hoodie pocket and brought out the old pencil case he'd been keeping the money in.

"Eighty-four dollars," Lauren said proudly as Sam emptied it onto the table.

Dad frowned. "I don't get it."

"We were going to adopt Bitsy ourselves!" Lauren explained. "I really, really don't want to give her to some stranger! We thought puppy stuff probably costs about $100, and we were so close to having it, and then that man came! We had to hide Bitsy in case he got her first!"

"Does this have something to do with the table full of apples at the top of the road?" Mom asked.

Lauren nodded. "We sold the apples from the orchard, and my old toys, too."

"And it's my birthday money."

"And my money from Grandma."

"There are more apples left," Sam added. "We should get to a hundred easily."

Mom smiled sadly. "That man drove all the way out here from Pine Hills. He really wants to adopt a beagle puppy and said he would be back tomorrow to get her."

Lauren started to cry. She was going to have to give up Bitsy after all.

Bitsy looked up from her bowl. What was the matter with Lauren? She dashed across the kitchen floor and scratched frantically at Lauren's legs.

Lauren reached down and picked Bitsy up, cuddling her close, while Sam petted her head.

Bitsy howled loudly, joining in with Lauren's sobbing.

"Lauren, shhh...," her dad said gently. "And please tell Bitsy to hush, too. I can't hear myself think. That's better," he added as Lauren petted Bitsy and shushed her. "We didn't realize you were that desperate to keep Bitsy. Why didn't you say something?"

"I tried!" Lauren burst out. "But you kept saying we had Baylee, and ever since the puppies came, you'd said we couldn't keep them. I told Sam about it, didn't I?"

Sam nodded. "But we thought if we had enough money we could keep her. Lauren said I could share her, too."

"Oh, Sam…," his mom said sadly. "He loves dogs," she explained to Lauren's parents. "But his dad is allergic."

Lauren's mom was watching Bitsy, snuggling up in Lauren's arms, her eyes switching from person to person, as she tried to follow what was going on. "She is beautiful," Mom said slowly.

Lauren's dad looked at her. "It was you who said no more dogs, Annie!"

"Somehow I can't imagine being back to just one after all those puppies. It already seems very quiet, with only Baylee and Bitsy." Mom smiled. "And she's definitely the prettiest of the litter."

"So can we keep her?" Lauren asked,

not quite sure whether that was what her mom was saying. "Really? You mean it?"

Mom nodded and laughed as Lauren hugged her, squishing Bitsy in between them. "Don't squash her!"

"But if Baylee has puppies again, we're not keeping any!" Dad said sternly.

Lauren shook her head. "Oh, no, I promise I wouldn't even ask!"

"You can have your birthday money back, Sam," Lauren's mom said, smiling.

Sam nodded, but he looked a little sad.

"Do you still want to share Bitsy, though?" Lauren asked, holding Bitsy out to him.

Sam nodded eagerly, and Bitsy wagged her tail so fast it almost blurred, and then licked his hand lovingly.

"We can use the apple money to buy her a really nice new collar and leash," Lauren suggested. "Not Baylee's old ones anymore. And we can put 'This dog belongs to Lauren and Sam' on her collar tag."

Everyone laughed, and Bitsy howled again, a real show-off howl with her ears thrown back and her tail wagging under Sam's arm.

Sam grinned. "I think she likes that idea."

The Abandoned Puppy

Contents

Chapter One
A Real Treat

The littlest puppy whimpered quietly. The cardboard box had stopped bouncing up and down, but no one had come to get her out, and it was still so dark. She didn't like it. She didn't know where her mother was, and she was hungry.

She squeaked in frightened surprise as a low rumbling noise shook the box. It seemed to be moving again, swinging and then sliding across the floor. Her two brothers slammed into her, knocking her against the side of the box as the car went around a sharp corner.

The journey seemed to go on for a very long time, but she couldn't even curl up to sleep. Every time she managed to get comfortable, the box would slide around again, and they'd all be on top of each other. It was nothing like their rough-and-tumble puppy play in the big basket at home. This hurt, and they couldn't go and snuggle up against their mother when they wanted the game to stop.

Pressed into the farthest corner, the puppy scratched anxiously against her

brothers. They were sitting on her again!
Then she realized that they'd stopped—
the box wasn't sliding around anymore.
Her brothers stood up cautiously. They
listened, flinching a little at the creaky
wheeze of the car trunk opening. Then
the box swung up into the air and was
dropped down with a heavy thud.

They heard footsteps hurrying away.
And then they were left alone.

"Are you ready to go, Zoe?" Aunt Jo was standing at the front door of their house, wearing her rain boots and her Redwood Animal Rescue fleece.

"Yes!" Zoe dashed down the hallway, stuffing the packet of dried apricots that Mom had found in the back of the cupboard into her lunchbox. She and Mom had both forgotten she'd need packed lunches this week, so Zoe's lunch was a bit random. Still, she really liked peanut butter and jelly sandwiches!

"Where's your older sister?" Aunt Jo asked, peering down the hallway into the kitchen.

"She's still asleep." Zoe shook her head. "Kyla thinks I'm crazy to get up early to come with you when I don't have to."

"Well, if you stayed at home with your sister all day, you'd just end up watching TV for the entire Easter vacation!" Mom called out. "You'll have a much better time at the rescue!"

"I heard that!" Kyla's voice floated down from upstairs. "I'm not asleep, and I'm not watching TV. I'm studying! In bed! See you later, Aunt Jo. I'll come and pick Zoe up."

Kyla had exams coming up, so she was studying as hard as she could. Zoe was really glad that Aunt Jo had said she could help out at the rescue—she normally only got to help out after school. It would have been boring being stuck at home with

Kyla, and Mom couldn't afford to take any time off work. Sometimes when they were off from school, she got to spend the day with her friend Becca, but Becca had gone to her grandmother's in Canada for two weeks.

"Thanks for letting me come for the entire day," Zoe said to Aunt Jo as they walked to the rescue, which was about 10 minutes from Zoe's house.

"That's all right!" Aunt Jo grinned at her. "I'm not going to be letting you off lightly, you know. I've got a long list of jobs for you to do, starting with cleaning out the dogs' runs, then bathing the cats, and maybe even knitting some bodywarmers for the guinea pigs...." She looked down at Zoe's worried face. "I'm just teasing you, Zo! There will be a lot of useful stuff you can do, I promise, but it'll be mostly exercising the dogs, if it's not too wet. They don't get walked as much on the weekends, because that's when we get most of our visitors. They'll all be desperate for a good run around the yard."

Redwood was a small rescue, but it took in every kind of animal. The staff did their best to get them all adopted, but it wasn't always easy. Aunt Jo had been working there for three years now, ever since she'd gone to the rescue to get a cat and come home with Boots, her handsome tabby. She had been working as a receptionist at the local vet back then. That's how she knew all about Redwood. She'd ended up volunteering to help out at the rescue in her spare time. Then, when a job had come up as manager, she'd jumped at the chance. Zoe had been delighted, too.

"You're so lucky, getting to be at the rescue every day, and seeing all the dogs," Zoe sighed. "I'm definitely going to work somewhere like Redwood when I'm older. Or maybe I'll be a vet," she added thoughtfully.

Aunt Jo smiled at her. "It's a great job at the rescue," she agreed. "But it does have its downsides, too. Sometimes it makes me so angry the way people don't take care of their animals properly. And it isn't always the owner's fault, either. Sometimes they really love their pets, but they just can't take care of them in the same way anymore. That's really heartbreaking." She sighed. "I just want to take them all home with me. But four cats is enough!"

Having just Boots the tabby hadn't lasted very long. Aunt Jo was a softie when it came to big, fluffy cats.

"So, did anybody take a dog or cat home over the weekend?" Zoe asked. She loved hearing about the new homes the animals went to. She liked to imagine herself into some of the stories Aunt Jo told. She would love to have a dog from the rescue, but she knew they couldn't. It wouldn't be fair to leave it all alone in their house while Mom was at work, and Kyla wasn't really a dog fan, either. She'd been chased across the park by a huge Bernese mountain dog when she was about four years old. She and Mom had been on their way to preschool, and Kyla had been on her scooter. The dog had only wanted to be friendly, but Kyla hadn't known that, and she'd fallen off trying to get away from him. She'd been scared of dogs ever since.

"Eddie got chosen this weekend!" said Aunt Jo. "Finally! I'm so happy,

Zoe. I thought he'd never find a home!"

Zoe grinned. Eddie was one of the older dogs—a bulldog. A lot of people seemed to think that they were weird-looking. Everyone always wanted a cute little puppy, but Eddie had such a sweet nature.

"An elderly man came in," Aunt Jo went on. "He wanted Eddie right away. He said that he'd always had bulldogs, and Eddie was perfect. One of the staff did a home visit, because Mr. Johnson was so eager to take Eddie right away. She said it looked ideal. A nice yard, and near a park for good walks. She figured Eddie and Mr. Johnson were a perfect match— both of them being on the elderly side. You know Eddie never liked walking very fast!"

Zoe giggled. She'd taken Eddie around the park with Aunt Jo and a couple of the other dogs from the rescue before. It was the slowest walk she'd ever been on!

"Lucky Eddie. And lucky Mr.

Johnson," Zoe said. "I bet they're having such a great time." She wrapped her arm through Aunt Jo's and leaned against her with a sigh. "I know we can't, but I wish I could have a dog of my *own*...."

Chapter Two
The Nighttime Delivery

The box seemed to be getting colder and colder. The April night had been frosty, and the puppies had huddled together to keep warm. They weren't used to being outside at night, and there was only the thin cardboard box between them and the concrete steps. They had always slept in their comfortable basket, snuggled up next to their mother. The cold was a frightening shock.

The smallest of the three, the tiny girl puppy, woke up first. She was miserably stiff, the cold aching inside her, and she scratched worriedly at the cardboard under her paws. Her two brothers were still asleep, curled up together, but somehow during the night, she had rolled away from them. Now she was on her own in the corner of the box, shivering and hungry.

She tried to scratch at the side of the box, wondering if she could get out and somehow find her way back to her mother.

But even her claws hurt this morning, and she felt weak and sleepy. Too feeble to claw a hole in the side of a box.

She still didn't understand what had happened. Why had they been taken away from their mother, and their warm basket? Was someone going to come and get them, and take them back to her? When they'd been put into the box, she'd heard her mother barking and whining—she hadn't wanted them to go any more than they had. The littlest puppy had a horrible feeling that they might not be going back.

Zoe and her aunt were almost at the rescue. Zoe could feel herself speeding up. She loved it when they got to be the ones who opened up at Redwood—it was a real treat and usually only happened if Aunt Jo let her come and help on a Saturday. She knew that all the animals would be excited to see someone after a night on their own. The dogs would be the most obvious about it, jumping around and scratching at the wire mesh on the front of their pens and barking like crazy. But even the cats, who usually liked to be more standoffish, would spring up from their baskets and come to see who was there. The rescue had a big pen full of guinea pigs at the moment, so there would be happy squeaking from them, too.

Aunt Jo was searching in her bag for the keys, so it was Zoe who first noticed that there was something strange on the front steps.

"What's that?" she asked curiously, frowning at what looked like a box in front of the main door to the rescue.

Aunt Jo looked up from the bunch of keys. "What?"

"There. On the steps. Maybe someone donated food to the shelter, Aunt Jo!" People did bring in pet food for the animals occasionally—Zoe had seen them. "It's funny that they didn't bring it in when there was someone who could say thank you, though."

"Hmmm…." Aunt Jo was walking faster now, the keys dangling forgotten in her hand.

"What's the matter?" Zoe asked. She could see that her aunt looked worried.

"People leave us other things, too, Zoe," Aunt Jo sighed. "It might be an abandoned animal in that box. If it is, I guess that at least they've brought it to us, but I hate it when they just leave it like that."

Zoe felt her eyes filling with tears. The box was just a box, a shabby cardboard one. How could someone stuff a cat or a dog in there, and then just leave it? It was so mean!

They hurried up the steps and sat down slowly, one on either side of the box. Aunt Jo took a deep breath. "I never get used to this," she whispered as she started to unfold the flaps on the top. "It's been such a cold night. Look, there's frost on the top. If there's something inside, I hope it hasn't been in there for long."

There was a feeble scratching noise from inside the box, and Zoe caught her breath. "There *is* something inside there!"

Aunt Jo frowned at the box. "Yes.

And I'm being silly, Zo. We should take the box inside. We don't want whoever's in here getting scared and leaping out."

Zoe nodded. "Good idea. Can I take it?" she asked hopefully. "You can unlock the door."

Carefully, Zoe slipped her hands underneath the box, shivering as she touched the clammy, cold cardboard. Whoever was in it must have had a miserably cold night. She heaved the box up and felt something inside it wriggle. There was a worried little squeak, and a yap.

"It's okay," she whispered. "We're just taking you into the rescue. It'll be nice and warm in there. Well, warmer than out here, anyway."

Aunt Jo had unlocked the doors now, and she was just turning off the alarm. She held the door open for Zoe, and they hurried into the reception area, putting the box down on one of the chairs.

"I think it's a dog," Zoe told her aunt. "I definitely heard a yapping noise. But it can't be a very big dog, because the box hardly weighed anything at all."

"Let's see." Aunt Jo lifted the flaps of the box—it was meant to hold packets of chocolate cookies, Zoe noticed—and they both peered in.

Staring anxiously up at them were
three tiny brown and white puppies.

Chapter Three
New Surroundings

The littlest puppy flinched back against the side of the box. She was still so tired from being bounced and shaken around, and now the light was flooding in, after hours of being shut in the dark. It hurt her eyes, and she whimpered unhappily. Her bigger, stronger brothers recovered more quickly, bouncing up to see what was happening, and where they were. But the little girl puppy pressed her nose into the corner of the box, hiding away from the light. She was too cold and tired to get up anyway.

Zoe and her aunt gazed inside, and Zoe pushed her hand into Aunt Jo's. She'd never seen such little puppies at the rescue. They were the smallest puppies she'd ever seen anywhere.

"Oh my goodness, three of them," muttered Aunt Jo.

"They're so tiny," Zoe whispered. "They can hardly weigh anything at all."

Aunt Jo nodded. "They're much too young to be away from their mother, really. They can only be a few weeks old. Great job keeping quiet, Zo. We don't want to scare them. They may not be used to seeing different people."

The puppies were looking up at Zoe and Aunt Jo uncertainly. One of the boy puppies scratched hopefully at the side of the box, clearly wanting to be lifted out.

"Well, he's not shy," Aunt Jo laughed quietly.

Very gently, she slipped her hands into the box and lifted out the puppy. He wagged his stubby little tail and licked her fingers. "Yes, you're a sweetheart, aren't you?" She turned to Zoe. "They must be starving

if they've been in this box all night.
Now that I can see him clearly, I don't
think this little boy can be more than
four weeks old. He's probably only just
been weaned from his mother. They
should be having four or five meals
a day, and a bit of their mom's milk
still."

Zoe giggled. "That's why he's trying
to eat your fingers…." Then she looked
worriedly down into the box. "Aunt
Jo, what about the little puppy in the
corner? Is she okay? She isn't moving
like the other two."

Her aunt sighed. "No, she isn't….
We'd better take a look at her. Can you
bring the box into one of the puppy
pens? Then we'll have somewhere
cozy for them to curl up, and we can

mix up some puppy milk."

Zoe gently lifted up the box, with two puppies still in it, and followed her aunt into the main rescue area, where all the pens were. Dogs jumped up excitedly as they came past, barking for their breakfast, and for someone to come and give them some attention. Zoe looked down worriedly at the two puppies in the box. The bigger one—she was pretty sure it was another boy—was now standing up, balancing carefully on plump little paws and listening to the new and exciting noises. He looked up curiously at Zoe—the only person he could see at the moment.

Maybe he thinks it's me barking! Zoe thought to herself, smiling down at him.

But her smile faded as she looked over at the other puppy. The tiny puppy was still curled miserably in the corner of the box. She didn't seem to want to get up and see what was going on at all.

"We'll put them in here—nice and close to the kitchen," Aunt Jo said, opening one of the pen doors and crooning to the puppy snuggled in the crook of her arm. "I'm pretty sure we've got a big tin of that powdered puppy milk replacement left," Aunt Jo continued. "And some of the bottles. I'd better order some more, though."

She sat down on the floor in the pen with the puppy in her arms, and Zoe put the box down next to her, kneeling beside it. "Should we take the others out?" she asked, looking at the boy puppy, who was clawing excitedly at the side of the box now.

Aunt Jo nodded. "Be careful though, Zoe. Don't scare them. They might not be very big, but puppies can still nip if they're frightened. Get the bigger puppy out first, then we can let him explore with this one, while we see what's the matter with the tiny one."

Zoe reached in and picked up the puppy, who was still standing up against the side of the box. He wriggled and yapped excitedly, and when she put him down on her lap, he squirmed around eagerly, trying to see everything in the pen. Then he nuzzled Zoe's fingers and wriggled carefully down the leg of her jeans, making for the floor. He obviously just wanted to go exploring in this new place.

The other boy puppy was still snuggled on Aunt Jo's lap, looking around curiously, but not quite confident enough to go marching around like his brother.

"Try just giving the little one a gentle pet," Aunt Jo advised. "Don't go right in and pick her up. She isn't looking at us, and she'd get startled."

Zoe reached in and ran one finger down the puppy's silky back. The brown fur was so soft, but she didn't feel as warm as her brother. "She's pretty cold," Zoe said, glancing at Aunt Jo. "Even just touching her. And she's sort of floppy."

Aunt Jo bit her lip. "She's suffered more being out all night because she's smaller. Here, put this on your lap, Zoe." She lifted a soft fleece blanket out of a padded basket in the corner of the pen. "Then lift her out carefully and wrap her up. Just loosely. And keep your hands around her to warm her up a bit."

Zoe nodded and gently cupped one hand around the puppy. The tiny dog shivered a little as she felt Zoe's fingers, and turned her head slightly. But she was just too weak to look up. Zoe slipped the other hand underneath her and lifted her out onto the blanket. She wrapped it around the puppy, petting her gently through the folds.

"Okay, little one," Aunt Jo said to the puppy on her lap. "I need to go and get your sister a hot-water bottle. And make some milk for you guys. Okay?

Want to go and see this nice basket?" She put the puppy in and petted him for a few seconds until he got used to being somewhere new. Then she got up slowly. The other boy puppy trotted over to the basket, too, nosing affectionately at his brother.

"Those two seem fine," she said, sounding relieved. "And I'm sure they'll be even brighter once they've had something to eat."

Zoe looked up at her. "What about this one?" Her voice wobbled. "You don't think she's going to be all right?"

Aunt Jo sighed. "We don't know yet. She seems very weak. I'm going to call Samantha at the vet and ask if she'll come over as soon as she can and take a look at them all. Are you okay with them for a minute while I get a hot-water bottle for the little one?"

Zoe nodded, still gently rubbing the puppy through the blanket. She wished she could feel her moving. The puppy felt like a saggy little beanbag, slumped on her lap. Carefully, she moved the blanket from around the puppy's head, looking at her face. Her eyes were closed, and her pink tongue was slightly sticking out of her mouth. *It looks dry*, Zoe thought worriedly. Aunt Jo had better hurry up with that puppy milk. She hoped they'd be able to persuade the puppy to drink it. She didn't look like she wanted to make the effort to do anything at the moment.

"Here's the hot-water bottle," Aunt Jo said, hurrying back. "I've wrapped it up so it isn't too hot."

"Do we put her on top of it?" Zoe asked, starting to lift the puppy off her lap.

"No, that would be too hot. I'm going to put it at the side of the basket, then she can snuggle next to it. We'll just have to keep an eye on her brothers and make sure they don't nudge her away."

"Maybe we should put her in a pen of her own," Zoe said doubtfully. "They're a lot bigger than she is. They might push her around."

"I'd rather keep them together if we can. She's already lost her mother, and her home. Her brothers are the only security she knows. Also, if we separate her, she might find it difficult to manage being around other dogs when she's bigger."

Zoe nodded as she laid the puppy close to the hot-water bottle. "We don't want her to be lonely," she agreed.

"I've started to warm up some puppy milk. I'll just go and get it, and we can see what they think." Aunt Jo ducked into the kitchen and came back with a shallow metal tray of the special puppy milk. "Hopefully they won't tip this over," she explained to Zoe, who was looking at the tray in surprise—it looked like something her mom would make brownies in.

The two boy puppies had been nosing

around the edges of the pen, trying to explore, but as soon as Aunt Jo put the tray down, they galloped over to see what it was—so fast that they got tangled up and fell over each other. They struggled to their feet, mock-growling, and then scurried up to the tray, sniffing at it excitedly. It only took seconds before they were eagerly lapping, burying their tiny muzzles in the milk and splashing it around.

"They must have had milk from bowls before," Zoe said, watching them and giggling.

"Maybe. Or else they're just fast learners," said Aunt Jo. "I don't think we need to worry about them not eating." But she was frowning. "I'd really hoped that the smell would wake the little one up, but she doesn't seem to have noticed. We'll have to try feeding it to her by the bottle."

Zoe nodded. "Should I put her on my lap?" she asked hopefully. She'd loved holding the puppy before, and trying to warm her up. Even though it was scary that the puppy was sick, it felt really special to be the one trying to make her better.

"Yes. Unwrap her, and we'll try to

get her to take a bottle. I brought one just in case." Aunt Jo took a baby's bottle with a cap out of the pocket of her fleece and sat down next to Zoe. "She's still so sleepy...."

The puppy was really floppy now, and she didn't wriggle when Zoe unwrapped her. Aunt Jo held the teat of the bottle up to her mouth, but she didn't seem to notice it. She certainly didn't start sucking, as Zoe had hoped she would. She only turned her head away a little, as though Aunt Jo nudging the bottle against her mouth was annoying.

"She doesn't want it," Zoe said worriedly. "Is there anything else we can give her?"

"We could try using a syringe...,"

Aunt Jo said thoughtfully. "We can poke it into the corner of her mouth and try and trickle it in." But Zoe could see that her aunt was doubtful about the puppy ever feeding at all.

"What about...." Zoe brushed her fingers against the teat, letting a few drops of milk ooze out of the tiny hole onto her fingers. It was thick and yellowish, not like ordinary milk at all. Holding her breath, she moved her milky fingers across the puppy's mouth, letting the milk run onto the dry, pink tongue.

The puppy shivered with surprise and the little tongue darted out, licking Zoe's fingers.

"She likes it!" Zoe squeaked.

Aunt Jo smiled. "You take the bottle. Squeeze a little out onto the end of the teat and dribble it into her mouth."

The puppy licked eagerly at the teat this time, and when Zoe pushed it gently against her mouth, she sucked, harder and harder, until she was slurping messily at the milk.

And then, at last, she opened her dark eyes and stared up at Zoe.

Chapter Four
Puppy Playtime

To: Becca
From: Zoe
Subject: Puppies

Hi Becca!

I hope you're having a good time at your grandmother's. I'm sorry I haven't e-mailed you in a couple of days. Been sooooo busy! I went to the rescue with Aunt Jo on Monday, and someone had abandoned three puppies in a box on the front steps!!! (Here's a picture. Aunt Jo took it on her phone. Aren't they beautiful?) We've named the two boys Brownie and Chip and the girl puppy Cookie. She's really pretty. When we first found them, she was really weak, and Aunt Jo told me afterward she wasn't sure she was going to make it. We're giving her milk from a bottle because she won't eat mashed-up puppy food and milk, even though her two brothers love it! (You should see them eating. It goes everywhere, and we have to wash them afterward!) But some of it must be going inside them—they're getting fatter every day! Cookie is definitely getting bigger, too, and she likes me to carry her around everywhere! I have a bunch more pictures that Mom printed out for me, so I'll show you when you get back.

Love, Zoe xxxxxxxxxxxxx

To: Zoe
From: Becca
Subject: Re:Puppies

Hi Zoe!

I can't believe you found puppies! You are so lucky. Grandma's place is okay, but it's a little cold since it's by the ocean. I went swimming and my toes almost fell off.

Will the puppies get new owners from the rescue? How old are they? I wish I could come and see them. Guess what? Mom and Dad say we can definitely have a dog (you know they wouldn't make up their minds before). But now they say we have to go slow and make sure we find the right dog! Aaargh! I really want to have a dog NOW! When I get back please ask your aunt if I can come and see the puppies. Maybe one of them could be our dog!!!

Love, Becca xxxxxxxxxxx

Zoe read Becca's reply to her e-mail, smiling to herself. Becca wrote e-mails just like she talked. But her smile faded a little as she read on to the end. Becca was so lucky to be allowed to have a dog. Zoe had been talking to Aunt Jo about the puppies today at the rescue. They'd been weighing them to check that they were eating enough, which was difficult because Brownie, Chip, and Cookie saw no reason why they should stand still on top of the scales, and just kept bouncing around. In the end, Aunt Jo had made a guess at their weights, but she said they were definitely getting heavier, which was the main thing.

Then they'd taken five minutes just to play with the puppies—it seemed like fun, rather than work, but Zoe knew it was actually really important. If the puppies didn't ever get played with, they wouldn't know how to behave with their new owners.

"How could anyone have abandoned them?" Zoe said sadly, watching Brownie and Chip zooming up and down the pen, chasing after a ball. Cookie was scampering after them, not quite brave enough or fast enough to take the ball from her brothers, but having just as much fun. "They're so perfect, all of them. How could anyone be so mean?"

Aunt Jo sighed. "Well, at least they brought them here. It was a start."

"But they left them out in the cold all night!"

"Some people just don't think. The puppies were probably an accident— they hadn't had the mom spayed, and then maybe the owners felt they couldn't afford to buy all the puppy food, and take the puppies to the vet for vaccinations. Dogs are expensive to own." She reached over to put her arm around Zoe's shoulders. "Don't think about it, Zo. The puppies were lucky they ended up here, so they've got all of us taking care of them. We're going to turn them into well-behaved dogs and make sure they only go to wonderful owners. They won't remember their horrible start."

"I hope not," Zoe whispered, with a tiny sigh. Aunt Jo's words were meant to make her feel better. She knew the puppies would need to leave the rescue in a few weeks, but she'd been trying not to think about it too much. She'd only known them for a few days, but they were so sweet, Cookie especially.

If they could stay at the rescue for a little longer, she'd be able to keep taking care of them…. But that wasn't fair. They needed forever homes.

Reading the exciting news in Becca's e-mail had made her think about having to say good-bye to the puppies all over again….

To: Becca
From: Zoe
Subject: Puppies

Hi Becca,

Aunt Jo thinks the puppies were about four weeks old when we found them, so now they're five weeks. They can't go to new homes until they're about eight weeks old. I'm sure you can come and see them! I'll ask Aunt Jo. You're so lucky to get a dog! I hope your mom and dad decide on one soon. See you back at school in a week!

Love, Zoe xx

It wasn't as friendly as her e-mails to Becca usually were, but Zoe was feeling sad. She stared at her computer screen, not really seeing the cute photo of Cookie that she had set as her wallpaper.

"What's up?"

Zoe jumped. She hadn't heard Mom come in at all. "Nothing…. I was just thinking about the puppies. I'm going to miss them so much when they get adopted." She gulped. "Especially Cookie."

Mom nodded. "She is beautiful." Zoe had shown Mom the puppies one afternoon at the rescue when Mom had come to pick her up. "I think it's her eyes. She has such a little face that it makes her eyes look huge, and then she has those beautiful whiskery eyebrows. Has Aunt Jo figured out what breed they are yet?"

Zoe giggled and shook her head. "Nope. Everyone at Redwood thinks they're something different. Aunt Jo thinks maybe there's some Jack Russell in them and maybe some Cockapoo, too. But we might not be able to tell until they're bigger. Almost grown-up. And we won't have them then, will we? So we'll never know." She sniffed, and Mom hugged her.

"But you knew they'd have to go to new homes, Zo! All the animals at the rescue do. You've never gotten this upset before."

"I know. Maybe it was because we found them—and feeding Cookie with the bottle has made her special to me, Mom." Zoe smiled proudly. "I got her to take some puppy food and milk in a bowl this morning. Aunt Jo was really happy—she said that she'd thought Cookie was going to have to be on bottles forever!"

"Your Aunt Jo should be paying you!" Mom sighed. "I know you love it at the rescue, but maybe you should have a couple of days off from helping out. Do something else. I bet Kyla could take a break from studying to take you shopping. Or to the movies?"

Zoe looked horrified. "Oh, no, Mom! I have to keep going. I have to help Cookie learn to eat the solid food. It's really important."

Her mom gave her a worried look. "Well, I guess so...."

Chapter Five
Becca's Visit

"It sounds like the best Easter vacation ever!" Becca sighed enviously.

Zoe smiled at her as they walked into their classroom. "It was awesome. I really missed going to the rescue this morning. I was looking forward to seeing you, but aside from that, I could have done without school!"

"Me, too, but I can't see my mom

letting me have the day off because I needed to go and visit the world's cutest puppies...." Becca flopped down into her chair and glanced at the board. "Multiplication problems! Great start to the new quarter...." She got out her math book but went on talking in a whisper. "So is Cookie completely weaned now? She's eating real puppy food?"

Zoe nodded. "Yup, they all still drink a little bit of milk, but they've started drinking water, too. And Cookie's really catching up with Brownie and Chip. I don't think she'll ever be as big as they are, but she's doing okay. I brought the pictures Mom printed out—I'll show you at recess—Shhh! Mrs. Allen is watching us." She stopped talking and tried to look like she was concentrating on the problems that Mrs. Allen had put on the board for them. Their teacher was usually a lot of fun, but she always got extra strict when they came back after vacation—as though she thought they needed to remember what school was like!

Zoe showed the pictures to Becca and some of the other girls in her class at recess, and everyone said how adorable the puppies were. Several of the girls said they were going to ask their moms and dads if they could come to the rescue and see the puppies, and maybe even adopt one of them. Zoe knew that most of her friends wouldn't be allowed to—Lucy already had two dogs at home! But the more people who came to see the puppies, the better. As much as Zoe hated the thought of the puppies leaving the rescue, she wanted them to have the very best homes.

That afternoon, Aunt Jo had arranged to pick Zoe up from school. Mom was going to get her after she finished work. Zoe got changed quickly in the bathroom—Mom hated it when she got her school uniform dirty—and then ran to see Cookie and the others.

Cookie was curled up in their basket, watching her brothers playing tug-of-war with a piece of old rope that someone had given them. They'd had it since the morning, and it was their new favorite toy. Pieces of it were scattered all over the pen. She sighed a little and rested her nose on her paws, wondering where Zoe was. Zoe had played with her every day since they'd come here from their old home. Actually, the little puppy couldn't remember much of where they'd lived before they'd been at the rescue. The only thing she was sure of was that their mother had been at the old place. She still wondered what had happened, and why they had been taken away, but she didn't mind, because now she had Zoe.

Except that today she didn't, and she didn't understand why. Zoe always fed her and her brothers. Zoe gave them a lot of attention, even though she wasn't drinking milk from her lap anymore. Zoe still brought the food bowls and watched to make sure that she was eating enough. Zoe even stopped Brownie and Chip from trying to take her food if they finished theirs first.

Today the other lady had brought their food—Jo, the one who was always with Zoe. Jo had said nice things, and she'd petted her, and said how good she was. But it wasn't the same.

Cookie's little ears pricked up sharply. Someone was running along the hallway between the pens— someone with small, light footsteps. She jumped up in the basket and barked excitedly as  Zoe appeared at the front of the pen, beaming at her.

"Oh! Did you miss me? I really missed you," Zoe told her, opening the latch. "You too, yes, I missed you as well, you great big monsters," she told Brownie and Chip, patting them lovingly as they circled around her feet. But it was Cookie that she sat down next to, and Cookie she cuddled as soon as the puppy clambered happily into her lap.

"I missed you more," Zoe whispered into her ears as she petted her. "I know I shouldn't really say it, but I did." She sighed. "There are some people who are going to come and look at you, Cookie. Try to look like a perfect pet, okay? You aren't old enough to go for a couple more weeks, but if they like you, they might wait."

She could hear them coming along the line of pens now—a couple, who'd just bought a house together, and were thinking of getting a dog. They'd said they didn't mind whether it was a puppy or an older dog, but when Aunt Jo had mentioned the three beautiful little puppies, they had gotten excited.

"They'll be looking for you." Zoe sighed again. "They looked nice, I guess. Nice-ish…." She couldn't imagine anyone being a good enough owner for her special Cookie. No one except her, she realized with a miserable little gulp.

"So they decided on Jasper?" Zoe asked as she helped her aunt to clean out the food bowls, feeling a bit surprised, but very relieved. Jasper was about five years old and was a mixed-breed, mostly Labrador. *He isn't as cute as Cookie and her brothers*, Zoe thought.

"Yes, they decided that they wanted a bigger dog after all," Aunt Jo explained. "Don't worry, Zoe. It won't be hard to find homes for those three at all. They're beautiful. It's the older dogs that can be hard to place."

Zoe nodded. "My friend Becca is going to get a dog soon. Becca said she'd love to come and see the puppies. She's going to ask her mom and dad if they could come this weekend. That would be okay, wouldn't it?" Her voice wobbled a little bit. "It'll only be one more week until the puppies are old enough to go to new homes then...."

Aunt Jo looked closely at her. "Yes, they'll be about seven weeks old this weekend, as far as we can tell. It won't hurt them to be split up from their litter after eight weeks. It would be wonderful for one of your friends to come. Zoe, are you okay, sweetheart?"

"I'll miss them, that's all," Zoe muttered.

"I know you will. Especially Cookie. You've taken care of her so well. But she can't stay here, Zo, you know that. It isn't a good life for a dog, in a little pen like this, no matter much we love them."

"I know. But it's hard to think of someone else taking her home. I wish we could have a dog! I'd take care of her so well!" Zoe burst out. Then she added quietly, "Don't worry, I know we can't…."

Aunt Jo hugged her, accidentally clanging two stainless steel dishes together behind her back, and making Zoe laugh.

"I'm so excited!" Becca raced up the steps toward Zoe, her mom following behind. She flung her arms around her. "Please can we see all the dogs? And the cats? I know we don't want a cat, but I'd like to see them anyway. And the guinea pigs!"

"I'll show you everything," Zoe promised, giggling. She hadn't seen her friend so hyper since her birthday party. She took them all around the rescue, saving the dog pens until last.

"You're so lucky, getting to help here all the time," Becca told her, cooing at the guinea pigs. Then she looked excitedly up at her mom. "Please can you show us the dogs now, Zoe? Mom and Dad said we might be able to get one really soon. That's what Dad's doing today—fixing our fence so that there aren't any holes around the bottom of it, and it's safe for a dog to be in the yard. He said if we found a dog from somewhere like here, the rescue would want to come and check that we'd take care of it well."

Zoe nodded. "Yes, Aunt Jo and the other staff go and look around everyone's houses. They wouldn't let you have a cat from here if you lived on a really busy road. Or if you had small children. You'll be all right," she added. "You want a dog, and it's only really small children that are a problem—you know, too small to understand about not pulling tails."

Becca nodded.

"Doesn't your dad want to help choose a dog?" Zoe asked curiously.

Becca's mom smiled. "This is just a first look—so we can think about what kind of dog we'd like. Becca's dad will come and see them if we tell him there's a dog we really like. But he started worrying about the fence last night, and he was determined to get it done. He didn't want us to miss out on a beautiful dog because the house wasn't ready."

Zoe smiled. It sounded as though Becca and her mom and dad were really serious about getting a dog. They weren't just deciding to adopt one without thinking it through, like some people did. "Okay, well, here are the dog pens. It can get pretty noisy!" she warned Becca as several of the dogs started to bark excitedly when they realized they had visitors.

"Oh, look…," Becca whispered, glancing from side to side. "So many!

Lulu, Freddie…. Oh, he's so handsome! Mom, look! He looks like a German shepherd. Oooh! Trixie!" Becca crouched down by the little spaniel's pen. "She's so pretty…."

She glanced up worriedly at Zoe. "How do people ever choose? She's looking at me, like she really wants us to take her home, and I haven't even gone halfway along the pens yet!"

"It is hard," Zoe admitted. "If you think you really like any of the dogs, tell me, and I'll ask Aunt Jo if you can go into the pens and meet them."

"If I did that, I'd never be able to say no," Becca's mom muttered. "What if we cuddled a dog and then said we didn't want him? It would be heartbreaking!"

Zoe wrinkled her nose. She supposed she was more used to the rescue than most people. "I know it's sad. But Aunt Jo and the others do find homes for all the dogs in the end. It takes a while for some of them, though." She led Becca and her mom along the row of pens. "And these…," she stopped by a pen, "are the puppies we found abandoned." She laughed as all three of them raced toward the wire of the pen. "The one with the darker brown patches is Brownie, and that one's Chip...." She pointed to the puppy with the brown eyepatch. "And this one, with the pale brown patches," she paused, "is Cookie."

"Oh, wow...," Becca sighed. "They're all so beautiful!"

"They are adorable," her mom agreed. "They look very little, Zoe. Are they old enough to be adopted?"

"Not for about another week," Zoe explained. "But then it will be fine, although they still can't go outside for a while after that. All the dogs in here have been vaccinated, but puppies have to have more vaccinations when they're about 12 weeks old. Then they can go for walks. They'd be okay in the yard, though," she added.

"You know a lot about dogs," Becca said admiringly. "Can we pet them? Mom, do you want to?"

Her mom nodded, smiling. "Definitely."

Zoe swallowed hard and opened the latch on the pen. It was a good thing that Becca and her mom liked the puppies. But it was one step closer to them leaving the rescue ... and Zoe.

Cookie scratched excitedly at the wire. Zoe had been playing with them that morning, and then she'd disappeared. Now she was back!

But there were other people, too. Another girl, like Zoe, and someone else. Cookie had never seen them before. She stopped wagging her tail quite so hard and backed up a bit as Zoe opened the door. She wasn't used to different people.

Zoe let Becca and her mom in, and Brownie and Chip sniffed cautiously at them. Becca picked up the last piece of the rope toy and wiggled it along the ground, right in front of Brownie, who quickly pounced on it, pretending to growl.

"He's so funny!" Becca giggled.

"I think he's the friendliest of the puppies," Zoe told her. She looked around for Cookie, who was almost hiding behind her, watching Becca and her mom with big, anxious eyes. "It's all right, Cookie," she whispered.

Cookie pressed herself against Zoe's side and sniffed cautiously at Becca's mom's fingers when she held them out. The new people smelled nice, but she didn't know them like she knew Zoe. She didn't mind if this lady petted her, though.

"She's very sweet," Becca's mom said. "Is this the one you bottle-fed, Zoe? You can see that she adores you."

Zoe smiled sadly. She loved that Cookie acted like her dog, even though she wasn't. She sighed. Cookie was going to have to learn to love somebody else. Gently, she lifted Cookie up and put her on Becca's mom's lap.

Cookie froze and sat motionless, her shoulders all hunched up under her ears. She looked around at Zoe worriedly, but she didn't wriggle off. It was all right. Zoe was still there, very close. The lady rubbed her ears, which was nice. She relaxed a little and licked her hand.

"She's a tiny bit shy, but she's very loving," Zoe said, trying not to mind someone else cuddling Cookie. She took a deep breath. "She'd be a wonderful pet. Any of them would."

Cookie watched sadly, her ears
flattening back, as they all got up. They
were going, she could tell. She missed Zoe
so much now that she didn't stay all day
the way she used to. Zoe had been here
for longer today, but Cookie still hadn't
had her snack. Cookie liked it when Zoe
brought her food and sat with her while
she ate. She always ate more when Zoe
was there, because Zoe liked to see her

eat, and she would tell her what a good dog she was, eating so nicely.

As Zoe was shutting the front of the pen, Cookie raced after her, scratching her claws against the wire netting and whining sadly.

"It's okay," Zoe whispered to her. "I'll be back tomorrow. I promise."

Cookie didn't know what that meant, but she understood Zoe's comforting voice. She stopped whining and just stood up against the wire, staring after the girls as they walked down the hallway between the pens. She watched until the doors swung shut and she couldn't see Zoe anymore. Then she dropped down and sadly padded over to their basket, her claws clicking against the worn tiles on the floor.

Chapter Six
A Difficult Week

"Mom says we can make pancakes for dinner!" Becca told Zoe happily as they took their coats off.

"I love pancakes," Zoe said, trying to sound more cheerful than she felt. It was a treat to go to Becca's house, but she would have preferred to stay at the rescue with Cookie and the others for a little longer. It would be rude to say that, though.

The girls curled up on the couch and watched a movie. Zoe was careful not to let herself think about how nice it would be if there were a little puppy snuggled up between them watching, too. But next time, there might be. Becca's dad was still outside fixing the fence. When they'd gotten back, he'd shown them the shiny new wire neatly running around the base of the old wooden fence. They'd brought him a cup of tea and a plate of cookies, and he'd said gratefully that he thought he was almost finished. It looked like their entire family was really committed to having a dog.

Becca had gone to get them both some juice, leaving Zoe watching the movie—they'd both seen it before—

and now she came running back in.

"Zoe! I've just been talking to Mom and Dad, and guess what!"

Zoe blinked at her in surprise.

"We're going to ask your aunt if we can reserve one of the three puppies! Mom's calling her now! She's arranging for them to come and do a home visit, too!" Becca was dancing around the room in delight, and Zoe stared at her.

This was good news. One of the puppies was going to have a wonderful new home and be well taken care of. Zoe would even be able to keep on seeing whichever puppy they chose. She'd know what the puppies would look like when they were grown up, after all!

But what if they choose Cookie? the voice inside Zoe's head whispered. Then Cookie would belong to someone else. She stopped herself. This was her best friend, Becca, that they were talking about. Cookie would have a perfect home.

"That's wonderful," she told Becca finally, swallowing back the lump in her throat. "Aunt Jo will be really happy."

"Oh, and Mom says dinner is ready," Becca added.

Zoe nodded. That was good. After dinner, it would be time for her to go home, and she wouldn't have to keep pretending to be happy for Becca. She knew that she should be, but she wasn't.

She was burningly, horribly jealous instead, and she felt terrible for it.

"We went out yesterday to that big pet store over by the supermarket. Have you ever been there?"

Zoe shook her head.

"I hadn't, either. It's enormous, and it sells everything! You'd love it, Zoe," Becca rambled on happily. "Your aunt e-mailed Mom a long list of stuff we'll need, and we even got some things that weren't on the list, just because they were so fun! A lot of toys! The puppies love playing with those toys they have in their pen at the rescue, don't they?"

Zoe nodded. "Yes," she muttered quietly, burying her head as she took her pencil case and book out of her bag.

"And we have to make sure that our puppy has a lot to do, because it might be lonely without any others to play with. Although I'll be there, of course. Zoe, are you okay?" Becca added. "You're so quiet."

"I'm fine." Zoe tried to sound enthusiastic. "Did you get a rope toy? The puppies really like that old piece of rope they've got."

"Yes! A beautiful one. Much nicer than that ratty old one they have now."

Zoe sniffed, trying not to cry. *But they like that ratty old piece of rope*, she thought to herself. *And what if Becca chooses Cookie?* Zoe stopped herself. Whichever puppy Becca chose was going to be so lucky.

I'd be a good owner, too, she said to herself miserably. *I know so much about taking care of dogs. I've fed those puppies, and cleaned up after them, and washed them when they got themselves covered in puppy food....*

"Did you hear me, Zoe?" Becca nudged her gently, and Zoe jumped.

"Um, no. I'm sorry. What?"

"I just said that we're going to go to the rescue on Saturday and choose the puppy, and then it can come home with us!"

"Oh!" *So soon!* Zoe swallowed hard. "That's great," she muttered. "Um, I'm going to the bathroom. Tell Mrs. Allen where I am if she comes, okay?"

Zoe tried as hard as she could to be her usual self with Becca that week, but it was so, so difficult.

Becca clearly knew that something was wrong. Zoe kept avoiding her, and dashing off to change her library book instead of chatting with Becca and their other friends at lunchtime. She spent the entire recess hiding in the bathroom one day after Becca started telling her about the beautiful collars she'd seen on a pet website. They had little pawprint designs woven into them, and space for a phone number, so that if the dog got lost, it was easy for someone to call you. It had just made Zoe feel too upset. She'd had to tell Becca she felt sick when the bell rang.

Zoe hated lying to her friend all the time, but she didn't want to admit how jealous and upset she was really feeling.

By Friday, Becca had stopped telling her about all the things they were doing to get ready for the puppy. She almost wasn't talking to Zoe at all. And at lunch, she went off and played with a group of other girls in their class without even asking Zoe if she wanted to join in.

"See you tomorrow morning, then," she told Zoe rather awkwardly as they put their coats on at the end of the day.

Zoe nodded. "Okay. 'Bye, Becca."

And that was that. No running out to the gate together. No promises to call later about homework. Becca just walked away, leaving Zoe fiddling with the zipper on her jacket and feeling totally miserable.

Kyla was waiting for her outside
school as usual—the high school was
just up the road from Zoe's school, and
she usually got out later than Zoe did,
but Zoe had taken a long time that
afternoon.

"Are you all right?" she asked. "You
look really down."

Zoe shrugged. "I'm sort of not talking
to Becca," she admitted. "It's horrible."

"Did you have a fight?" her sister asked sympathetically.

"No." Zoe sighed. "It's all my fault. You know the puppies at the rescue?"

Kyla laughed. "No, Zoe, it's not as if you've ever talked about them at home."

Zoe swung her schoolbag at her sister, making a face. But Kyla was always good at cheering her up. "She's going to adopt one."

Kyla smiled, and then looked confused. "But that's good, isn't it?"

"Yes," Zoe said in a small voice. "I just wish I could, too, that's all. I'm jealous…. And worse than that, I'm worried that she might choose Cookie."

"Oh, Zo…." Kyla hugged her. "I haven't met these puppies, but I can see how much they mean to you.

Why don't we stop off at the rescue so you can show me them?"

"But you hate dogs!" Zoe stared at her.

"I don't hate them." Kyla shrugged. "I think I'm getting better. One of my friends at school has a really cute spaniel. I even let him sit on my lap on the couch the other day."

"Wow, Kyla! That's great!" Zoe smiled. "Of course I'll show you the puppies. You're going to love them, especially Cookie—she's beautiful. I was going to ask Mom if she could take me over there later, but let's go now." She grabbed Kyla's hand and practically pulled her down the road.

"All right, all right, take it easy!" Kyla grinned.

It didn't take them long to walk across

the park toward Redwood, and soon they were turning into the driveway.

"I brought Kyla to see the puppies!" she told Aunt Jo as they popped their heads around the office door.

Aunt Jo looked up from her computer. "Hi, Kyla!" She grinned. "That's great news."

"Hi, Aunt Jo." Kyla smiled back. "I just thought I'd like to see them. Mom said they were really cute."

"They are." Aunt Jo nodded. "I'll call your mom and tell her you're both here. I can take you home in the car if you'd like."

"That would be great," said Zoe. "Come on, Kyla—they're down here." Zoe grabbed Kyla's hand and pulled her down the hallway. "Don't worry. I don't think there are any really big dogs in the rescue at the moment," she added, seeing her sister glancing cautiously into the pens.

"I just don't like it when they jump against the wire," Kyla whispered.

"Brownie and Chip do jump up, but they're really little," Zoe promised. "Cookie won't, not until she's figured out who you are, because she's a little shy."

"Okay. Oh, Zoe, are these them?" Kyla stopped in front of the puppies' pen, smiling at them delightedly. They were all asleep, for once, flopped in a sort of puppy pile in their basket. The pile heaved and wriggled every so often, and as Zoe gently undid the front of the pen, the pile struggled apart and turned into three hairy, whiskery, brown and white puppies who bounced happily around Zoe's feet.

"Do you want me to bring one of the puppies out?" Zoe asked. "Then you could pet just one—you wouldn't have them jumping all over you."

Kyla nodded, and Zoe picked Cookie up. Cookie nuzzled at her happily. She'd been hoping that Zoe would come soon. She looked around curiously as Zoe carried her out of the pen, leaving her two brothers behind, looking rather jealous. Cookie stared down at them, wagging her stubby little tail.

Zoe was carrying her to another girl, a taller girl with the same dark hair and eyes. Cookie looked at her with her head to one side—she looked very much like Zoe. But she didn't seem to be confident with dogs the way that Zoe was. She was looking nervous, and as she put out her hand, she patted her very quickly, as if she thought Cookie might bite.

Curious about this girl who looked so much like her favorite person, Cookie wriggled in Zoe's arms, stretching toward the other girl.

"She likes you!" Zoe said laughing.

"Does she?" Kyla asked, sounding surprised, and happy.

"Yes, she does," said Zoe. "Do you want to hold her?"

"I don't know...." Kyla looked uncertain. "Okay, let me try."

Kyla nodded slowly, then let Zoe put Cookie into her arms.

Cookie snuggled up against Kyla's chin, and slowly, Kyla petted her ears. The little dog closed her eyes.

"Oh, Zoe, she's beautiful." Kyla smiled down at the puppy. "No wonder you've been spending so much time here."

"She is, isn't she?" Zoe sighed sadly. "And now I just can't bear to think of letting her go...."

Chapter Seven
Decision Time

Cookie scampered around on the grass, chasing after the jingly ball. It was her favorite toy. She loved the noise it made, even though she didn't quite understand where the noise came from. It was definitely hers—Zoe had given it to her. It was the only toy she bothered to fight over.

Chip raced past her and dove onto

the ball, rolling over with it with his paws, and growling excitedly.

Cookie let out a sharp, furious bark and jumped on top of him, scrambling to get the ball back. Unfortunately, Chip was still quite a bit bigger than she was, and he wriggled and growled. Then somehow he was sitting on top of her instead, and he had the ball in his teeth now. He shook it backward and forward, still growling, so that it jingled like crazy.

"Stop fighting you two!" Zoe ran over. "Chip, Chip, look! Stretchy bone! Your best bone! Come on! Where's it going?"

Chip sprang up, dropping the ball, and danced around in circles as Zoe waved the blue rubber bone. Then she flung it across the yard, and he galloped after it like a racehorse.

Cookie seized her ball gratefully and sat down on Zoe's feet, panting.

"You really love that ball, don't you?" Zoe reached down and picked her up. "Look, there's a nice sunny patch over there. Let's just sit and watch those two brothers of yours being silly...."

It was a beautiful, warm May day, and Zoe had shorts on for the first time that year. She should have been feeling happy, but all she could think about was Becca. She'd be here soon. Which puppy would she choose? Zoe ran her hand gently down Cookie's back, over and over, as Cookie shook the ball gently back and forth, listening to the jingly noises.

"What if she chooses you, Cookie?" Zoe whispered. "I've been trying not to think about it. It was bad enough just thinking about Becca having a dog, and me not being able to have one. But what if it's actually you that she wants to take home with her?" She sighed and leaned over, resting her cheek against Cookie's soft fur for a moment. "At least I'd still get to see you. That's if Becca ever talks to me again, considering the way I've been acting this week. I've been awful."

Cookie looked at her for a moment, her eyes dark and sparkly. She licked Zoe's hand.

"Thank you!" Zoe grinned. "Was that to tell me you don't think I've been awful? I have, though. I was horrible, actually. I just can't tell if it would be worse to never see you again, or to see that you belong to someone else! I don't know whether to hope that Becca chooses you or not." This time Zoe heaved a huge sigh, so that Cookie turned around and stared at her. "I'm sorry! Did I shake you up and down?"

"Zoe!" Aunt Jo was calling her. "Becca and her mom and dad are here! They're just getting out of their car. Go and say hello. I'll bring these three in."

"Oh! Okay." Zoe gently put Cookie down, and the puppy scampered off after the ball again. She walked slowly through the rescue to the reception area, where Becca and her parents were now talking to Susie, who was at the reception desk.

"You two can chat while we fill out the paperwork," Becca's mom told them, smiling.

Becca couldn't have told her mom how grumpy Zoe had been all week, Zoe realized gratefully. "Hi…," she said timidly to Becca.

"Hi." Becca stared at her, and then

she pulled Zoe over into the corner, as if they were going to look at photos on the wall of the dogs and cats who'd been adopted recently. "Zoe, is there something going on?" she asked. "Are you mad at me?"

Zoe turned red and looked at her feet. "No … I…." She didn't know what to say.

"You are!" Becca cried out. "You've been acting really weird all week! What is it? What have I done?"

Zoe sighed. "Nothing. Nothing at all. I know I've been acting weird, but it isn't your fault. It's me. I've been jealous … jealous because you were getting a dog, and I couldn't have one, not ever. We don't have anyone at home to take care of a dog, and Kyla hates them anyway. I'm so sorry I've been horrible."

"Oh, Zoe." Becca gave her friend a big hug. "Why didn't you tell me?" she asked her, stepping back, her eyes round with surprise. "I'd have understood!"

"I suppose I just felt silly. And mean," Zoe muttered. "And I didn't really want to talk to you about it. You were so excited…."

Becca sighed. "I didn't think about it making you sad," she admitted. "Did I go on and on?"

Zoe gave a very small giggle. "Yes. All the time."

A voice behind them interrupted the awkward moment. It was Becca's dad.

"Are you girls ready?" he asked them. "I want to see these wonderful puppies you've been telling me about!"

Becca looked anxiously at Zoe, but Zoe nodded, managing to smile and look almost as though she meant it. "Come on!"

They walked down the hallway to the puppies' pen. Zoe spotted Aunt Jo coming back in from the yard with the puppies in her arms. "There they are," she told Becca's dad, pointing. "They've been playing outside."

The puppies saw them, too, and started to wriggle excitedly. Aunt Jo laughed and crouched down, letting them run down the hallway toward the visitors.

Cookie dashed ahead, streaking toward Zoe on her tiny little legs. Zoe was desperate to pick her up and cuddle her. But she couldn't. It was Becca's turn.

But Becca wasn't looking at Cookie, Zoe realized. She'd crouched down and was holding out her arms. Chip was running straight up to her, and now he was standing up on his hind legs, his front paws on her arms, giving happy, excited little barks. He licked her cheek and jumped as though she was the best thing he'd ever seen!

"He remembers me!" Becca cried delightedly. "I've only met him once, but he really remembers me! Oh, Dad, do you like him? His name is Chip, and he's the best one of all. Can we please take him home?"

Chapter Eight
Cookie's Perfect Home

Zoe watched, smiling, as Becca hugged Chip. He wriggled delightedly in her arms. So it would be a stranger who would be taking Cookie home, she realized sadly. She wouldn't see her adorable little puppy grow up into a beautiful dog after all.

Cookie patted her paws hopefully at Zoe's leg, asking to be picked up.

She could tell that Zoe was sad, but Cookie knew that she could make her feel better. When Zoe lifted her up at last, Cookie stood up in her arms, rubbing her whiskery nose against Zoe's cheek. That always made her laugh.

"You're so pretty," Zoe told her, but she didn't sound much happier.

Cookie watched interestedly as the girl cuddling Chip gave him some crunchy treats, then carefully lifted him into a box, which was like a small pen with a wire front. She shivered a little, burying her nose in Zoe's neck. It reminded her of the box they'd all been closed up in. It felt like a very long time ago now.

Chip looked confused, and whined, but the girl fed him some more treats through the wire, and then the man with her picked the box up and carried him down the hall to the door.

Cookie gave a little whimper of surprise. They could go away? Chip was going with that girl, and the other two people? She didn't understand. If they were allowed out of the rescue, why didn't Zoe take her when she went? Maybe she would! Maybe they were all going! Cookie's tail started to flick back and forth with excitement.

"Well, that was good, wasn't it?" Aunt Jo said, sounding really happy. "And I meant to tell you, Zoe, a really nice-sounding family called me asking about puppies, and they were interested in getting a boy puppy—so that would be you, Brownie." She looked down at the puppy in her arms, who'd barked when he heard his name. "Yes, you! They're going to come and see you tomorrow, aren't they, sweetie? So we're getting there."

Zoe nodded. So that would leave just

Cookie. And she wouldn't be there for much longer either, Zoe was sure.

"Oh, look, there's your mom and Kyla," Aunt Jo pointed out, and she turned to open the front of the pen and put Brownie back in.

Zoe sighed and walked toward the pen to put Cookie in, too. She'd forgotten that Mom was coming to pick her up early. She wanted them to go and do some shopping— Zoe needed new school shoes. Zoe had tried arguing that Mom could just buy them for her, but Mom had said no.

Cookie twisted in her arms, struggling frantically, and whining. She wasn't going back in the pen—she wanted to stay with Zoe! Someone had already taken Chip away. Only Zoe could take her.

"What's the matter?" Zoe gasped, holding the puppy tightly and backing away from the pen, as that seemed to be what was upsetting her.

"Is Cookie okay?" Mom asked worriedly. She and Kyla had just come into the hallway between the pens, and now she was hurrying toward Zoe.

"She got really upset when I was trying to put her back in the pen." Zoe cuddled Cookie close against her shoulder. She could feel the little dog's sides heaving; she was shaking so badly. "Maybe she's sad about Chip going."

She wrinkled up her brow. "It's okay, Cookie. It's okay," she whispered. But then her eyes filled with tears. "I'm telling her everything's going to be all right, but it isn't," she said miserably, looking between Aunt Jo and Mom. "Chip has gone to a new home, and Brownie will probably go, too, tomorrow, and then it'll be just Cookie left. And someone will choose her really soon, and we'll never see her again."

Aunt Jo frowned. "I wonder if she does know what's happening. Some dogs really do seem to understand, much more than you'd think they could. Maybe that's why she doesn't want to go back into that pen."

"But she has to," Zoe said dismally. "What are we going to do? Do you think she'd be better if we moved her into a different pen?"

Aunt Jo glanced at Mom and shook her head. "No, to be honest, I think it would just be better if she went back with you."

"But then it would be harder for her to come back here." Zoe blinked, not really understanding what her aunt was saying.

"Or we could keep her," her mom said, putting an arm around Zoe's shoulders and gently patting Cookie.

Zoe looked puzzled. "But there's no one to take care of her in the daytime."

Her mom glanced at Aunt Jo. "We've been talking about that. I told your aunt I was worried about how much you were falling in love with Cookie. That you were going to be really upset when she went to her new home."

"And I said you were so good with dogs that you really deserved to have one of your own," said Aunt Jo.

"So we've come up with a plan," said her mom.

"I'm going to have her here at work with me in the day, Zoe," Aunt Jo explained. "She can have a basket under my desk, and I'll take her for a walk at lunchtime."

"And Kyla?" said Zoe, flashing her sister a look.

"I don't feel scared around Cookie,"

said Kyla. "She's a little sweetheart. Mom told me how much you'd bonded with Cookie— it was actually my idea that we should have her. That's why I wanted to meet her last week."

"Really?" Zoe stared at them all, her eyes like saucers. "You mean it? We can have Cookie? So—so we could take her home now?" Zoe whispered, hardly daring to hope that they'd say yes.

Aunt Jo smiled. "Well, she obviously doesn't want to go back in that pen. I can stay here and give Brownie a lot of attention so he doesn't mind being on his own. And you can borrow some food bowls and things until you can get your own."

Zoe nodded, thinking how much allowance money she had saved up, and how she was going to spend all of it at the pet store on the little puppy. Cookie was going to have the nicest things she could find.

"You're coming home with us," she whispered to Cookie. "You really are."

Cookie nudged Zoe's cheek with her damp black nose and looked hopefully at the door.

"Look at them! They're having such a good time," Zoe said, laughing at the two little brown and white dogs—Chip and Cookie. Who would have thought it? They were standing at the bottom of a huge tree, right at the end of their extending leashes. And they were both jumping up and down, barking like crazy.

"I wonder if Brownie likes chasing squirrels, too," Becca said thoughtfully. "Maybe we'll see him in the park one of these days."

Zoe nodded. "I bet he does. And I bet he never catches them, either."

The squirrel was sitting high up in the tree now, looking down at the two dogs in disgust. They hadn't come anywhere near getting him, and he clearly wasn't very bothered. He almost looked like he was yawning.

Eventually, Cookie and Chip gave up on the squirrel and wandered back to Zoe and Becca.

"Cookie's catching up with him," Becca commented. "She's almost as big as he is now. She might even end up being bigger!"

"Maybe," Zoe agreed. "They probably won't finish growing until they're about nine months old. Maybe even a year. They're four months old now, so they've got five months more growing to do, at least. You're going to be a huge dog one day, aren't you?" she told Cookie affectionately, crouching down and rubbing her ears and petting her back.

Becca giggled. Cookie might get bigger one day, but she and Chip were still tiny at the moment. Not that they seemed to think they were little at all. They strutted through the park as though they thought they were the most important dogs there.

"They wouldn't fit in that box now," Zoe said suddenly, looking up at Becca.

Becca shook her head. "I still don't know how someone could have left them like that. But I'm just glad it was you and your Aunt Jo who found them."

Zoe nodded, scratching Cookie under the chin, so that she closed her eyes blissfully, and her tail thumped on the ground.

"I know. Me, too."